'You're a tiny little thing, aren't you?

'Small and beautiful and quite exquisite,' Hunter continued. 'A lone little angel sent into the big bad world.'

'Very amusing.' Angel glared up at him determinedly, even as she registered that he was the sexiest man she'd ever met.

'There's just one thing missing... Your wings.'

He was laughing at her, mocking her name, she thought furiously. 'How do you know angels have wings?'

'Oh, they do. But then maybe you're a fallen angel...?'

Dear Reader

Welcome to our exciting mini-series—**Sealed with a Kiss**. Every month we'll be featuring a romance sparked off by a letter, an advertisement, or even a diary. Some of the world's greatest romances have begun in writing...and ended with a marriage licence! This is a tradition continued by ten of our popular authors—each and every one of whom has brought her own unique style to the romance.

We hope that you enjoy this **Sealed with a Kiss** title and all the other terrific romances that we have out this month!

The Editor

P.S. Look out for next month's **Sealed with a Kiss** title - INVITATION TO LOVE by Leigh Michaels

ANGELS DO HAVE WINGS

BY
HELEN BROOKS

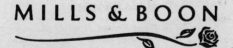

MILLS & BOON LIMITED
ETON HOUSE, 18-24 PARADISE ROAD
RICHMOND, SURREY TW9 1SR

First published in Great Britain 1994 by Mills & Boon Limited

© Helen Brooks 1994

Australian copyright 1994   Philippine copyright 1995 This edition 1995

ISBN 0 263 78814 8

Set in Times Roman 11 on 12 pt. 01-9501-48268 C

Made and printed in Great Britain

CHAPTER ONE

Dᴇᴀʀ Vicky,

Absolutely thrilled to hear you got a First in chemistry and biology—all that hard work paid off in the end, eh? Now that you're really on your way to being a doctor, how does it feel? And I want no more talk about feeling guilty when you write me your news—it was my own decision to leave university when I did and take care of Toby when Mum and Dad died; no one twisted my arm, and I don't regret it for a second. He won't be twelve forever and in a few years I can take up my studying and still try for a degree and medical school. I love to hear from you, really—it keeps me in touch with what I used to be.

Things are just the same here, of course; nothing ever happens in Braybrook that's worth mentioning. If there's one thing that *is* certain, that's it. My life is mapped out for years ahead without a chance of anything changing and I have to admit—but only to you—I do find that a bit hard at times. But it's good for Toby; he really needs consistency and security more than anything else. I must close now or I'll be late for work; I just wanted to write as quickly as I could

and tell you how very pleased I am at your brilliant news. Take care and write again soon.
Love, Angel.

As Angelina folded the single sheet of paper slowly and slipped it inside the envelope, the pangs of envy that had been paramount since receiving Vicky's letter early that morning began to subside. She was glad for her friend, she was, and her turn would come one day...maybe. No, *not* maybe. She thumped the stamp on the envelope with unnecessary vigour. It was up to her, after all, and she would *make* it happen. It was no use crying for the moon now, but when the chance came to don a space-suit and claim it she would be there.

She nodded to the empty room. She had always wanted to work in a hospital, either in a laboratory or, if her aptitude went that far, as a doctor, and there was no need to give up the dream, merely postpone it for a while. The last eighteen months had been hard, very hard, but Toby was happier now and things were improving each week. But, oh...she caught her breath in a little sigh as she glanced round the small kitchen filled with sunshine...if only things weren't so totally predictable, so boring and humdrum!

'Angel! Angel!' Angelina heard her brother's shrill cries seconds before he burst through the back door, scattering mud and grass off his shoes with scant disregard for the newly cleaned floor. 'Quick!'

'Toby!' She indicated the debris indignantly. 'I've told you time and time again, wipe your feet before you come in, and I thought you'd left for school any-way——'

'I said quick!' He advanced further, leaving more muddy footsteps. 'There's been an accident.'

'An accident?' Now he had all her attention as she sprang up from the kitchen table, brushing the thick fall of golden-blonde hair out of her eyes as she did so. 'Where?'

'Just outside.' Toby was pulling her towards the back door now, his young face desperate. 'I was running for the school bus and——'

But his sister had passed him at a trot through the open door, running round the side of the old stone cottage and down the overgrown path into the country lane beyond, where she suddenly stood stock-still so abruptly that Toby cannoned into her back.

'Oh, no!' She stared wide-eyed at what remained of her small, faithful Mini crushed between the thick stone wall that enclosed their property and a brand-new and very smart Range Rover. 'I don't believe this.' The other vehicle hardly had a mark but the driver, a well-built man in his late thirties, stood glowering at her as she approached him, for all the world as though *she* had driven into *him*.

'How on earth did you manage to do that?' she asked angrily as she came within speaking distance. It was too much, coming as it had on top of Vicky's letter that morning. Suddenly the difference in the way their lives had branched was magnified a hundred times. The world was Vicky's oyster, whereas she—— 'I'd parked it half on the verge as it was,' she continued testily as she bit back all thoughts of that other life. 'There was enough room to get a tank past if you'd driven properly.'

'If I'd *driven* properly?' In the split-second before he spoke Angelina just had time to register a pair of very dark grey eyes that shone like cold steel, and a hard mouth set forbiddingly in a square, tanned face. A rugged, masculine face. 'Now just hang on a darn minute——'

'Look what you've done to my car!' The ferocity in her vivid blue eyes made up for what she lacked in inches, her petite five-foot-two-inch frame at a definite disadvantage against his own superior height. 'What are you, anyway, some sort of speed freak?'

'Angel, please listen...' Toby had been hanging on her arm for the last few moments, trying to attract her attention, but now she shook him off angrily, turning her glare back to the tall figure in front of her.

'What speed were you doing, to lose control like that?' she asked furiously as her glance moved again over the sad remains of her little car. True, it had been ancient and hardly worth anything, but it had been a gem of a car, starting first time whatever the weather and never letting her down. She'd never be able to afford anything else; the insurance money would be a pittance. 'I can't believe——'

He stopped her with a cold, authoritative wave of his hand, his eyes icy. '*You* can't believe?' he said tightly. 'Well, somehow it doesn't worry me too much what you can or can't believe, Miss...?'

'Murray,' she finished tensely, her eyes flashing blue sparks at his total lack of remorse. 'Angelina Murray.'

'And this is?' He indicated Toby with another autocratic wave of his hand that made Angelina want to kick him.

'My brother Toby.' She eyed him furiously. 'Now what about my car?'

'You are most fortunate that it is merely the car that came off worst,' he said icily as his gaze fastened back on her hot face after one scathing glance at Toby skulking behind her.

'Fortunate?' She stared at him as though he was mad. 'You've just written off my car and you talk about my being *fortunate*?' She was conscious that her voice had risen to an unflattering shriek, but in the face of his overpowering arrogance all her normal cool self-control had gone up in flames. 'Well, let me tell you, Mr Whatever-your-name-is, we rely on that car for our very existence. How do you expect me to get to work——?'

'How you get to work, Miss Murray, is not my problem.' The cold grey eyes flicked grimly in Toby's direction again. 'However, if I hadn't swerved when I did, your brother's death might well have been. What have you got there, a complete idiot?'

'How dare you?'

'Oh, I dare, Miss Murray,' he said cuttingly. 'When someone takes it into their head to leap in front of my car from nowhere I dare do a lot of things. One of them that I'm doing battle with right now is the urge to teach that young fool a lesson he will never forget.'

She took a long look at the cold, sardonic face and big, powerful body and instinctively drew Toby further behind her. 'You lay a finger on him and you'll regret it.' Her voice wasn't as firm as she would have liked it to be but the venom in her blue eyes was enough to convince the devil himself that she meant what she said. 'He's only a boy.'

'Of twelve, thirteen . . .?' the caustic voice asked derisively. 'More than old enough to have some road sense, wouldn't you agree?'

'Toby?' She turned round so that her body was shielding Toby from the stranger's deadly gaze. 'What happened?'

'I was late, sis.' Toby looked up at her miserably, his big hazel eyes that were the very image of their mother's tragic. 'I've missed the bus twice this week already and Mr Williams would murder me if I was late again. I just didn't see him.' He moved a limp hand in the direction of the big, silent figure. 'It was my fault,' he finished lamely.

'Too damn true it was your fault.' The icy voice cut into the air like a knife. 'You nearly killed yourself, you could have killed me, and you've smashed up two vehicles in the process.'

'Hardly.' Angelina was conscious that she had handled this situation very badly right from the start but somehow, in the face of this man's supreme male arrogance, all thoughts of conciliation were totally absent. 'It's my car that's a write-off; yours is practically untouched.'

'Well, I do apologise,' he drawled sarcastically, his grey eyes chips of stone in the dark, weather-beaten face. 'Next time your brother decides to play his little games, perhaps it might be a good idea to have your car somewhere else? That way you can rest in peace knowing that, although he might kill the poor idiot at the wheel, or himself, your vehicle will remain untouched.'

'I didn't mean it like that and you know it,' she snapped back quickly. There was a hard lump gathering in her chest as the full realisation of what could have happened slowly dawned, but no way was she going to break down in front of this un-feeling brute. 'I'm very sorry that Toby was so stupid,' she continued flatly after taking a swift pull of air to quell the shaking that was threatening to become visible. 'I'll pay any expenses, of course.'

'Damn the money.' He eyed her with something akin to amazement darkening his eyes. 'Don't you realise that at this very minute your precious brother might be lying under those wheels?' He pointed to the expensive tyres on the shining Range Rover. 'Or would that be acceptable as long as your damn car was all right?'

'That's a despicable thing to say,' she said shakily as her eyes widened with shock.

'Yes, it is,' he agreed instantly, his jaw tight-ening. 'I apologise.' As she nodded slowly, he looked over her head in the direction of the cottage. 'Do I take it you live there?' he asked quietly, the grey eyes moving over the overgrown, untidy front garden in which hollyhocks, lupins and pansies vied with knee-length grass, thistles and tall, spiteful nettles. Her decision to give Toby as much quality time as he needed day by day had meant something had to go.

'Yes.' At the look on his face she drew up her head proudly. 'It is.'

'I see.' Just what he saw she wasn't sure, but as the dark grey gaze moved back to her face she was suddenly aware, with a little start of surprise, that she was looking at one of the most attractive men she had ever seen. And she was also *doubly* sure that she had never taken such an instant and profound dislike to anyone in her life. He was dressed casually but expensively, his jeans, trainers and shirt all the best that money could buy, and if she wasn't mistaken that was a solid gold watch gleaming on one tanned wrist. And the Range Rover was a beauty. He was clearly wealthy and powerful, with the arrogance to match. Strangely, the thought did not intimidate her; in fact just the opposite. As her small jaw jutted outwards and her back stiffened, the grey eyes watching her so carefully narrowed slightly, but other than that the tanned face remained imperturbable.

'Are your parents at home, Miss Murray?' he asked tightly after a long, strained moment of silence when they stared grimly at each other. 'I'm already late for an appointment.'

'No, they are not.' She cautioned Toby, who had stirred behind her, with a warning wave of her hand. 'But as I am over twenty-one and the car is mine there is no need to involve anyone else.'

'You're over twenty-one?' The grey eyes were frankly disbelieving. 'How much over?'

Normally the surprise people expressed when her age was revealed didn't bother Angelina an iota; she was more than aware that she didn't look a day over seventeen—she had been told it often enough! But the sceptical distrust in that cold, cynical face had her fists clenching into tight balls at her sides, and the blood pounding in her ears as though she had just run a race. 'I'm twenty-three, actually,' she said as calmly as she could considering the circumstances. 'Almost twenty-four.'

The heavy dark eyebrows disappeared into the shock of thick black hair at he whistled slowly through his teeth. 'I don't believe it.' It was a statement of fact, not surprise.

'You don't believe it?' she said coldly. 'Well, somehow it doesn't worry me too much what you can or can't believe.' As she parroted back the insult he had offered earlier, she saw him stiffen slowly as the words registered, and felt a second's intense satisfaction that she had pierced the armour. 'Nevertheless, I *am* twenty-three years old and more than used to dealing with my own affairs as I see fit. If you can wait a moment, I'll go and get my licence and insurance particulars, OK?'

He nodded silently, standing back a pace and watching her with cold, inscrutable eyes as she swung round and left him, almost dragging Toby behind her.

'How *could* you, Toby?' As soon as they had turned the corner of the cottage and were hidden from view Angelina rounded on Toby as a combination of rage, humiliation and relief had her gasping for words. Rage at the stranger's pretentious hauteur, humiliation at the position she had put herself in by jumping in before she had tested the water, and relief that Toby was alive and uninjured. 'All the times I've told you to be careful, to look both ways——'

'I know, I know.' Toby's face was white, his eyes enormous. 'I'm sorry, sis, really.'

She saw that he was desperately trying to fight back the tears, his bottom lip trembling, and somehow after all the tears he had cried in his twelve-year-old life that fact alone magnified the disaster. And the loss of the car *was* a disaster, whatever that supercilious six-footer outside said. It was obvious he had never had to worry about money in his life; wealth and influence just oozed out of every pore. Well, some of us were born with the normal metal spoons in our mouths, she thought grimly as she bent down and pulled Toby into her, the silver variety being in limited supply.

'I'm sorry, Toby, you must be all shaken up,' she whispered quietly into the blond head pressed against her chest. 'And at least you'll never do that again,' she added with a vain attempt at lightness as she kissed the golden hair softly.

'But the *car*?' Toby drew away and glanced up at her again, his face tragic. 'How will you get to work? And the shopping and everything?'

'Don't worry.' She smiled down into his freckled face with much more confidence than she was feeling. 'It might not be as bad as it looks. Dave might be able to mend it.' Dave Brown was the local mechanic from the small garage a few miles away, but she doubted that even he could work a miracle on the wreckage she had seen. 'Anyway, the important thing is that you're OK.' She hugged him again tightly as her heart shuddered in thankfulness.

When she joined the driver of the Range Rover again he was leaning against the big machine, his eyes hooded and his expression closed. As she approached, he waved a piece of paper lazily, straightening up as she reached his side. 'I think I've covered all the relevant details but my London address and telephone number is there along with my weekend place. I've recently bought the Gables on the outskirts of the next village. Do you know it?'

Of course she knew it. There wasn't anyone in a radius of fifty miles who didn't know the Gables, a magnificent Victorian mansion standing in its own grounds, complete with lake and tennis courts. And he'd bought it as a *weekend* retreat? She glared up at him without realising what she was doing. She'd been right: definitely a silver spoon. And she would bet her last penny he was a film director, or millionaire entrepreneur or maybe some slick, smooth-talking mogul of the less than honest variety.

'It was a simple question.' She came to with a jerk to find that the grey eyes were icy. 'Why did it provoke such wrath?'

'It didn't.' She forced her eyes away from his, lowering her head so that her heavy fall of thick blonde hair hid her face from his piercing gaze. 'I'm just a bit upset, that's all.'

'You and me both, Miss Murray.' The cold voice wasn't giving an inch as he waved disparagingly towards the cottage. 'Do I take it the instigator of all this trouble is skulking indoors?'

'If you are referring to Toby, he most certainly is *not* ''skulking'',' she said furiously as her head snapped upwards so violently that she felt her muscles scream in protest. 'I've asked him to make an important phone call for me, as it happens; we aren't all in the fortunate position of being able to please ourselves whether we work or not,' she finished tightly.

'Meaning?' he asked grimly.

'Let's put it this way, Mr...' she consulted the paper she had taken from him '...Mr Ryan. I would imagine that this Range Rover is not your only vehicle?' She stared straight into the cold grey eyes, her own blue ones vitriolic.

'What has that got to do with anything?' he asked roughly, a thread of curiosity colouring the deep voice.

'Everything.' She placed small hands on her rounded hips. 'Well, you haven't answered my question.'

'I wasn't under the impression I particularly had to,' he drawled coolly after a long moment of silence when he surveyed her from a face suddenly blank of all expression. 'But, since you ask, no, it is not my only vehicle. I have another car.'

'Which is?'

He leant back against the Range Rover again, the bright sunshine turning his black hair midnight-blue. 'A rather exclusive sports car, as it happens—a Lamborghini,' he said, slowly, mentioning a name that made her eyes widen, 'and, before you ask, it cost a hundred and fifty thousand pounds.' The grey eyes were dark, narrowed slits. 'It has a low, sloping windscreen, excellent instrument pod and I happen to like its aggressive and somewhat brutal appearance. Is there anything I've missed?' The deep voice dripped sarcasm.

Aggressive and brutal? She looked at the lean body in front of her, the strong, virile thighs and wide shoulders, and a little shiver snaked down her spine. She had never seen the car, only heard of its name, but it seemed tailor-made for its owner.

'It's also extremely beautiful, and I appreciate beauty, Miss Murray.' The dark voice was drawling now, and as the narrowed eyes flickered over her small, pale face, in which the dark violet-blue of her eyes stood out in luminescent contrast to the smooth, creamy skin, something in his expression made her take an involuntary step backwards. 'When linked to elegance and refinement, of course, and basic good taste.' His mouth twisted mockingly. 'You do know about good taste, of course, in spite of having a lamentable lack of it yourself?'

'And of course you're an expert on the subject?' she asked frostily as her skin burnt scarlet.

'I get by.' He smiled coolly, the dusky slate eyes as chilly as cold stone.

'Yes, I just bet you do.' It was crazy to provoke him further—suicidal—but there had been something burning away in her from the minute she had set eyes on him and she was powerless to resist its force. He was so very self-possessed, so utterly contemptuous of the world around him that it fired all her worst instincts. 'But then money is a great leveller of all the rough places, don't you find? I doubt if you have a clue how the other half live.'

'I've known a lot of women in my time but I can honestly say I've never met one with such an attitude problem,' he said grimly. 'You might look as though butter wouldn't melt in your mouth but that's as far as it goes, isn't it?' He moved towards her and she forced herself not to flinch or show any emotion as he stood in front of her, his big body blocking out the sun. 'Don't you like men, Miss Murray—is that it?' He let his eyes roam over her body in a manner that could only be termed insulting. 'If so, it's a chronic waste of good pleasure-time.'

'How dare you?' She glared up at him angrily. 'Is that how you view women? As chattels for your enjoyment?'

'Chattels?' He reached out a hand and grasped her hair at the back of her neck, drawing her head backwards with a subtle, unrelenting pressure that forced her face upwards. 'An old-fashioned word for a lady who is anything but. How many hearts have you broken, Miss Murray, with that gorgeous ripe little body and angelic face? How long did it take them to reach the acid underneath?'

'You're mad.' She tried to wriggle free but the hand at her neck tightened instantly.

'Probably.' He viewed her with cold thoughtfulness. 'It's certainly a long, long time since I let anyone get under my skin the way you have, anyway. That's almost a compliment, if you care to look at it in that way.'

'I don't.' She had ceased to struggle; it was pointless after all, and she wasn't going to give him the satisfaction of proving his superior strength. 'Not from a man like you.'

'A man like me?' He lifted his other hand, stroking her burning face gently with one long finger. His skin was smooth as it touched hers, sensitive, certainly not the rough, hard hands of a man who earned his living by honest physical toil.

But then most men in that position didn't own country mansions and houses in London, did they, she thought furiously, or strut around like the original feudal baron and drive the sort of sports car that was guaranteed to send women weak at the knees? But not this woman—oh, no. In fact she considered his particular form of boasting distasteful. She ignored the warning voice in the back of her mind that reminded her that she had instigated the information about the car—almost dragged it from him.

'Tell me, Miss Murray.' He was so close now that she felt his clean warm breath fan a wisp of hair across her cheek. 'What exactly do you know about men like me?'

'Enough.' There were ripples of sensation shooting down her spine now, making her legs go weak and her stomach shaky, but she would rather have died on the spot than let him suspect he was intimidating her. 'You're just a bully, the sort of vile bully who likes to threaten and shout. There was no need to be so antagonistic——'

'No need?' His eyes had narrowed into slits of grey and now his hand was like a steel vice. 'From where I was standing I had every right to be annoyed. Some idiot had just leapt in front of my car, causing me to swerve into a stationary vehicle or run right over him, and then disappeared, to return a few seconds later with a crazy harridan breathing fire and damnation. What the hell did you expect me to do? Present you with a bouquet and ask for a rerun? I could have killed the little fool——'

'But you didn't.' The sensations that were trickling through her body were most peculiar, she thought dazedly in a little separate compartment of her mind that seemed to be looking on as an interested spectator. He really was the most overwhelming man...

'And no thanks to him.' He glared down at her angrily. 'What are your parents thinking of, to let him run wild like that?'

'He wasn't running wild,' she said tightly as the reference to her parents caused an involuntary flinch. 'He was actually *running* for the school bus.'

'Couldn't you give him a lift?' Again as she tried to move there was that tightening of his hand that meant he wasn't finished with her yet. 'There can't be much for you to do in the mornings except pretty yourself up for whatever it is you do.'

'You pompous swine.' She was too angry to consider her words or the precarious position she was in. 'You know nothing about me or what I have to do.'

'That works both ways, Miss Murray, but it didn't stop you jumping to conclusions about me, did it?' There was no inflexion in his voice, no emotion at all, but she sensed nevertheless that he was furiously angry with her, and the sudden calm after his rage was distinctly unnerving. 'But I guess you'd argue that's different?' He eyed her cynically. 'Like most of your sex, you can twist any circumstances round to suit you.'

'Would you please let go of me?' She stared up at him defiantly.

'No.' Even as he answered, he moved her into his hard body in a way that was both intimate and shocking. 'I don't think I will.'

'Look, this is ridiculous——' Her words were cut off as his mouth descended on hers in a kiss that was fierce and sensual, and, although she beat her fists against his back as she struggled wildly in his arms, she might as well have been fighting solid stone. Part of her couldn't believe it was happening. This was the sort of thing that one read about in the papers, and which usually happened after dark in an ill-lit street or shadowed car park, not at half-past eight on a normal working day outside her own front door.

After a long moment he raised his head slowly to stare into her dazed blue eyes. 'You taste as good as you look,' he said huskily. 'What a pity that all that wonderful packaging hides the original twenty-four-carat shrew.'

And then she was free, standing swaying slightly in the warm spring sunshine at the abruptness of it all as he strode back towards the Range Rover, the continuing impact of his lips on hers effectively silencing all reaction.

The roar of the powerful engine broke the spell his assault on her defences had woven, but by then it was too late. Other than chase the big vehicle down the lane in an undignified pursuit that could only have one conclusion, she had no choice but to watch it disappear into the distance with its obnoxious owner thinking he had won. And he had! She ground her teeth in impotent rage. Damn him—he had.

CHAPTER TWO

ANGELINA was still standing staring wildly down the deserted dusty lane, framed by dense old trees rooted in verges covered with carpets of bluebells, when Toby joined her some minutes later.

'Sis?' He touched her gently on the arm, his blond hair a cap of gold in the clear morning light. 'Are you all right?'

'Not really.' But then she turned and saw his worried face and smiled in spite of herself. 'But you are, and that's all that matters. Promise me you'll never do that again, Toby—I don't know what I'd do if anything happened to you.'

'I promise.' There was a pinched look to his face that stopped the little lecture she had been about to give on the Green Cross Code, and she eyed him anxiously as they walked back to the cottage arm in arm, their faces turned by unspoken mutual consent away from the small battered car against the wall. She'd noticed that look more than once over the last few months, normally at the end of a hectic day when the small face had taken on an exhausted, drained appearance that didn't seem quite right for such a young child.

'*You* are all right, aren't you, Toby?' she asked carefully as they re-entered the small kitchen. 'There's nothing wrong?'

'No.' As he flopped down in a vacant chair the unease intensified. 'Well, there's the car.' He glanced up abruptly. 'Do you really think it's mendable?'

'I'm not sure,' she prevaricated quickly. 'Perhaps. But we'll manage somehow anyway; we always do.'

Her brother nodded glumly. 'I phoned Dr Mitchell to tell him you'd be late and he said not to worry, Shelly will stand in till you get there.'

'Right.' Angelina stared at him quietly. 'Well, I guess we'd better see about getting you to school. We'll have to walk down to the crossroads and catch the next bus from there. I'll come in with you and explain and then come back to the surgery.' Unfortunately Toby's school was situated some fifteen miles away in a large country town, the big brick building accommodating various children from the outlying districts and villages, but as there was a special bus which picked him up each morning at the end of the lane and dropped him off every evening that normally wasn't a problem. Unless he missed it.

Angelina worked as a receptionist-assistant in the local doctor's surgery a few miles down the road in the opposite direction to Toby's school, sharing the duties with another local girl, Michelle, known as Shelly, who had a small terraced house three doors away from the surgery where she lived with her husband and children. She had been very fortunate to get the job, work being scarce in the small village, and even more fortunate that she got on like a house on fire with Michelle, the two standing in for each other whenever necessary and even babysitting for each other when the need arose.

Dr Mitchell had been an old friend of her father's and was quite content to let the two girls work out the rota themselves as long as everything ran smoothly. Which it normally did. But not today, Angelina thought grimly as she hurried into the surgery nearly two hours later, hot and breathless. Definitely not today.

'Problems?' Shelly looked up from the appointment book with a sympathetic smile.

'And how!' Angelina grimaced her frustration. 'I've had a morning to end all mornings.'

'Tell me later.' Shelly nodded towards Dr Mitchell's closed door. 'There's some bigwig in there with him—a famous heart specialist from London. He's just asked for coffee and I've mixed up these appointments somehow. You couldn't...?'

'Sure.' Angelina made for the tiny kitchen at the back of the house. 'I'll make one for us while I'm about it.'

She stood looking out through the leaded kitchen window into the small, immaculate garden as she waited for the kettle to boil. Braybrook was the sort of picturesque old-world village that adapted very well to chocolate boxes, a bewitching little place of ancient stone cottages, ivy-clad walls, gardens full of hollyhocks, wallflowers and sweet-smelling, velvet-petalled roses and lazy lanes shaded by tall trees whose upper branches were thick with the nests of vociferous rooks. Angelina had lived there all her life and she loved it, but by the time she had started university some three years before she had been more than ready to leave. The quiet, sleepy village was charming and wonderfully rich in atmosphere, but the old medieval coaching inn that was now the local pub was the only entertainment of sorts for miles around. She had worked for almost eighteen months serving in a pharmacy in the town where Toby's school was situated before leaving for university in order to build up some capital for the three-year degree course to supplement her grant; her father's meagre wage as a farm worker was just enough to keep a roof over their heads and food in their mouths.

And then all her plans had come crashing down about her feet. She shut her eyes for a moment as the pain, still as fresh as when she had first heard about her parents' death, flooded through her body. It had been a freak accident, a chance in a million, the experts had said, but the old faulty gas fire that had leaked its deadly fumes into her parents' bedroom while they slept had robbed her and Toby of the best parents in the world. She bit on her lip hard as her eyes opened again. And so she had left university after only sixteen months and come home to Braybrook to enable Toby to stay in his own environment in the home he loved. She had looked upon it, and still did, as the last thing she could do for her parents, and she did it willingly out of a heart full of love for them and her young brother. But the last eighteen months had been hard financially and emotionally, the nightmares that had rent Toby's nights, shadowed with the horror of finding his parents dead, only just beginning to fade in the last few weeks.

The shrill whistle of the boiling kettle snapped her eyes to the task in hand, and when she emerged from the kitchen a few minutes later, with a pretty tray on which reposed the coffee-cups, a plate of biscuits and a small vase of yellow primroses from the surgery garden, her eyes were only very faintly shadowed.

'Take it in,' Shelly whispered as she reached out for their two cups and placed them on the old battered table they used as a reception desk. 'And I warn you, he's not your average sort of heart specialist. Name's Hunter, I think.'

Angelina raised enquiring eyebrows as Shelly pushed her towards the closed door, but her friend knocked and then ushered her through with the loaded tray without elaborating further. She had taken several steps into the room before the large figure sitting with his back to the door in one of Dr Mitchell's huge winged armchairs turned around, and when he did it was sheer reflex action that enabled her still to hold on to the tray.

'Good grief!' From the stunned expression in the grey eyes he was as surprised as she. 'What on earth are you doing here?'

'I work here.' She was operating on automatic as she continued to move across the room and place the tray on Dr Mitchell's polished desk, overwhelmingly grateful when it was safely out of her hands and she could hide their shaking behind her back. 'And I thought you said your name was Ryan?'

'It is.' He stared at her blankly. 'Hunter Ryan.'

Hunter Ryan. *Hunter* Ryan. Why hadn't she recognised his name this morning out on the road? He was one of the most eminent heart surgeons in the world, in spite of being a comparatively young thirty-nine. But there were hundreds of Ryans in the world and he hadn't written his first name, only the initial 'H'. But Hunter Ryan? Here?

'I don't like to interrupt this little scenario, but do you know my receptionist, Hunter?' Dr Mitchell raised enquiring eyebrows as they both turned to him as one, having totally forgotten his presence.

'This is the…young lady I was telling you about.' The brief hesitation before 'young lady' told Angelina more adequately than words what his description had been like.

'The one who was so rude?' Dr Mitchell asked tactlessly. 'Angel? I don't believe it.'

'Well, I'm sorry, Roger, but it's the same female.' Hunter's voice was faintly mocking now and full of lazy amusement. 'Unless you have a twin sister?' he asked silkily as he looked up at her again with those devastatingly piercing eyes.

'No.' After the first rush of horrified surprise there had followed breath-stopping panic, hot embarrassment and a wish that she were anywhere in the world but in this small room with these two men. But now, curiously, in the face of his undeniable mocking male arrogance and subtle sexual self-confidence, she felt the rage he had inspired earlier flood her system again. 'It was me. And if I was rude it was because you were even ruder.'

'Angel——'

He interrupted Dr Mitchell's obvious admonition with sardonically raised black eyebrows and a cold, taunting laugh. 'Angel? Her name's Angel? You've got to be joking.'

'Angelina Murray, actually, but you already know that, don't you?' She glared at him furiously. 'It's on the piece of paper I gave you when you wrote off my car this morning.' She saw Dr Mitchell shut his eyes for a fleeting second as though in horror, but there was nothing she could do about it. Famous heart specialist or not, the man was a pig. A rich, renowned and almost legendary pig, but still a pig.

'You certainly don't improve with further acquaintance,' he said coolly, the square, hard-boned face imperturbable. 'Twenty-three or not, your parents could do with teaching you a few manners.'

'Hunter——' She heard Dr Mitchell's anxious interruption but spoke before he could continue, her eyes blazing.

'Is that so?' she asked tightly, two spots of scarlet burning across her high cheekbones. 'Well, let's just say my opinion of you hasn't gone any higher either. You might be a good surgeon, Mr Ryan, but I for one thank my lucky stars I'll never have to find that out for myself. Your bedside manner must leave a hell of a lot to be desired. And my parents did an excellent job with me and Toby, incidentally, so you can keep the nasty remarks to yourself.'

She was out of the door again before either man had time to react at all, shutting it behind her with surprising quietness in the circumstances and marching past Shelly, whose smile died at her white face, and through into the small kitchen at the back.

'Angel?' Shelly had followed and her voice was anxious. 'What on earth is it?'

'Nothing.' She was concentrating very hard on quelling the storm of emotion that was rising in her chest. She hadn't cried when her parents died—she couldn't; she had had to be strong for Toby who had been a physical and emotional wreck from shock and grief. There was no way she was going to let this hateful man upset her; she *wouldn't*. She bit down painfully on her bottom lip until she tasted blood. She couldn't let go now; she had to be tough, capable, in control. Toby relied on her. She had to hold everything together. 'Nothing, Shelly.' She aimed for a weak smile that didn't quite come off. 'It's a long story. I'll tell you over coffee if you want to fetch the cups through.'

By the time she had finished relating the morning's events Shelly's mild brown eyes were wide with a mixture of interest, sympathy and agitation. 'Angel...' She shook her head slowly. 'None of that was like you at all. What came over you?'

'I don't know.' Angelina stared at her miserably. 'But he's such a loathsome man, Shelly; I've never met anyone I dislike as much as him.'

'I don't like to leave you here,' Shelly said uncomfortably, 'not after all that, but I've got to pick Robin up from the nursery at one.'

'Of course—you go.' Angelina nodded quickly. 'It was so good of you to stand in for me like that, Shelly. I'll do your shift tomorrow morning, of course. You go, don't worry, I'll be fine.'

'But are you sure he won't——?'

'Miss Murray?' As both women swung round, it was to see Hunter Ryan standing in the doorway, his grey eyes slightly narrowed as they fastened on to her pale face into which hot colour was already surging, but otherwise the dark features were betraying no expression at all.

Had he heard their conversation? Angelina glanced at the enigmatic male face warily. There was nothing to indicate that he had, but then she had the feeling that this particular male would be a whiz at poker. Those distant, cold features were quite unreadable. She hoped he hadn't come to engage in further hostilities. She would give as good as she got, *of course* she would, but the shaky feeling in her stomach and fluttering weakness in her limbs were rendering her more vulnerable than she would have liked.

'Could I have a word with Miss Murray in private, please?' The deep voice spoke directly to Shelly, who glanced nervously at Angelina before she left with obvious reluctance, her eyes worried.

'Yes?' Once they were alone Angelina forced herself to stare straight at him, annoyed that as usual her small stature let her down. He was a good eight or nine inches taller than she, and it was incredibly galling to have to put her head back so far in order to hold his gaze. She had always envied

tall women, but never so much as right now. It was
hard to have to admit to herself that he intimidated
her...but he did. Intimidated, threatened, and
yet—— There was something else too, a dangerous
ache of excitement, as unfamiliar as it was un-
welcome. He was so vigorous, so intensely alive and
in control of both himself and the circumstances
around him.

And the maleness of him... She caught her breath
in fascinated horror at the direction her thoughts
had taken. It was a dominating, sensual force, a
live entity that brought her eyes helplessly to the
powerful shoulders and hard, lean body as she
thought how it had felt to be moulded into that
dangerous male frame. And in spite of his contempt and dislike of her he had been aroused. That
much the close contact with his thighs had made
unmistakably plain, she remembered faintly with a
burning face.

'I had no idea of your circumstances when I
spoke about your parents in there.' He flicked his
head back in the direction of Dr Mitchell's room.
'Roger's explained the position you were forced
into——'

'Not forced.' She interrupted him quietly but with
unmistakable firmness as she surreptitiously wiped
her damp palms against the material of her skirt.
'I'm where I chose to be.'

He nodded recognition of her point. 'I'd like to
apologise for my less than tactful comment,
anyway,' he said stiffly. 'It was unnecessary and
uncalled for.'

She inclined her head in acceptance of the apology as she felt her skin burn even hotter. Hunter Ryan. *Hunter Ryan*! He had been like a god to some of the medical students she had been at university with, a brilliant and unorthodox surgeon who had followed his own perverse star against the advice of older and less wayward consultants and succeeded against all the odds. And she had thought he was a suspect businessman or disreputable entrepreneur! It would be funny if it weren't so awful. She *never* made snap judgements, not normally. But her emotions didn't seem to be normal around this man. Even now, when he was being so stiltedly correct, there was a strange kind of challenging aggressiveness about him that sent her pulse racing and tightened her lower stomach into one giant ache.

'Let's forget it, shall we?' she said as coolly as she could. 'And in case you're wondering, I am insured, by the way. There'll be no difficulty in meeting your expenses for the Range Rover.'

She raised her head as she spoke, and as their eyes met and locked his face darkened ominously. 'Is this the coals of fire treatment?' he asked coldly. 'Because if it is you can forget it. You were damn rude this morning with no justification at all——'

'And I suppose you acted like the perfect gentleman,' she shot back tightly, 'mauling me about like some adolescent teenager?'

'Mauling you?' The almost comical expression of outrage on the rugged face suggested it had been a long, long time since any woman had objected to his lovemaking—and why would they? Angelina thought grimly. He was famous, wealthy, successful and clearly had an ego to match. She knew how it was with these men within medical circles and in their own hospitals. They were treated with such deference and admiration that even the best of them developed a narcissism, a self-importance that was jumbo-sized unless they had someone in their private lives to keep their feet on solid ground. Was he married? She gazed at him defiantly as her thoughts raced on. If so, then his wife did nothing to balance that monstrous egomania.

'Yes, mauling me.' Her glare matched his. 'Or maybe you imagined I would *like* being grabbed by a total stranger and made to submit by brutal force?'

'I *kissed* you, for crying out loud,' he ground out harshly. 'Anyone listening to this conversation would imagine it was nothing short of rape.'

'It was, of a kind,' she persisted angrily. 'Certainly of my will and right of choice. I didn't want you to kiss me, Mr Ryan; I didn't want you to *touch* me! You are everything I dislike in a man, if you really want to know.'

'Loathsome was the word you chose, I think?'

So he *had* heard her conversation with Shelly? Well, it was his own fault, she thought tensely even as a dart of shame flicked through her. Right from the first second they had met he had been out to confront, subjugate and subdue, and she was blowed if she was putting up with such high-handed treatment. She remembered his furiously cold glare as she had walked towards him that morning before they had even spoken. He had probably perfected that with the hundreds of minions under his command!

'You weren't supposed to hear that,' she said tightly, 'but as you did...'

'It fits,' he finished grimly. 'What a little sweetheart you are!' The tone was acidly contemptuous.

'And we all know how you deal with "sweethearts".' She stared into the arrogant eyes angrily. 'Are we going to have another repeat performance of what you term "a kiss"?'

'Miss Murray, I wouldn't touch you with a ten-foot barge-pole even if you went down on your knees and begged!' he said icily. 'Goodbye.'

When the sound of his muted footsteps on the thin cord carpet covering the passageway outside had faded, Angelina found she was holding her breath until it began to hurt, and, breathing out in a long, hard sigh, she sat down very suddenly on one of the kitchen chairs as her legs finally crumpled. The urge to cry, to give way, was there again, and she fought it fiercely with all her might.

Why on earth had she said all that? Acted like that? She stared blindly at the wall opposite as the rapid beat of her heart seemed to fill her ears. She had never considered herself naturally aggressive; in fact all through her younger years her school reports had repeated the criticism that she needed to be more assertive and bold, that her tender heart and sensitive nature made her too susceptible as a general dogsbody to her friends and the class in general. If only those teachers could have seen her in action today, she thought painfully. The proverbial worm turning, in fact. She shut her eyes tightly, only to open them again quickly as male footsteps sounded just outside.

'Angel?' Dr Mitchell's grey head appeared enquiringly round the door. 'Is everything all right, dear?'

'Fine.' She stood up abruptly. 'Just fine.'

The rest of the day flew by, aided by several cups of strong black coffee and the flow of adrenalin that coursed through her body every time she thought of Hunter Ryan. Try as she might to stop it, her traitorous mind kept returning to the incident when he had held her trapped in his arms as his mouth had plundered hers. That a man in his position, a respected, esteemed position, could act in such a scandalous way was shocking, absolutely disgusting, she thought hotly as the smell and feel of him surrounded her for the twentieth time that afternoon, despite all her efforts to keep her senses under control.

She felt her skin grow warm as she remembered the feeling of vulnerability, of fragility, that his hard, masculine strength had induced. For the first time in her life the full promise of her femininity had been exposed, and it had been frightening . . . and exciting, her mind finished honestly. She brushed an errant strand of hair from her flushed face, confused and annoyed by her own feelings.

Since her first tentative awareness of the opposite sex at the age of fifteen she had had several boyfriends, none of whom had lasted more than a few weeks, and not one managing remotely to stir her blood. In fact if she was honest the main emotion they had produced in her had been one of faint irritation at their continual preoccupation with holding or touching her at every opportunity, and a feeling of regret that she couldn't feel for them what they obviously felt for her. They had all seemed so young, so juvenile, so intense. And, since returning from university to look after Toby, the daily grind of caring for the house, dealing with the shopping and household chores, being mother and father to a disturbed young boy and holding down a job they needed desperately to continue living in their home, had taken every minute of the day and night. There was never enough time.

She remembered Hunter Ryan's cutting glance as it had swept over the neglected garden, and bunched her hands into fists at her side. No doubt *he* had an army of gardeners ready to jump at his command, but she did not, and how *dared* he criticise her home? Not that he actually had, of course, in so many words. She bit on her lip crossly. But that cold, sardonic face had said it all. Oh, she hated the man, really hated him.

By the time she left to catch the one and only bus that patrolled the surrounding district on a two-hourly basis she was emotionally and physically exhausted. It was five o'clock on a damp and chilly spring evening, the sunshine of the day a distant memory now; she was tired, hungry and no nearer to finding a solution to how to survive the daily routine without her beloved little car. She had used the last of her savings to buy the little Mini after Dr Mitchell had offered her the receptionist's job a few weeks after she had returned home, and it had been a life-saver.

'Hi, sis.' Toby was sitting on the old stone wall waiting for her as she walked up the shadowed lane some twenty minutes later. 'Where's the car gone?'

'The car?' She stared vacantly at the blank spot where her Mini should have been. 'The *car*?' As her voice rose to a shriek the sound of a powerful engine approaching brought her head swinging round in the direction she had just come. It couldn't be, not now, but if it was she would hit him, kick him, *anything* if he said just one word out of place! And her car? Surely the police wouldn't have removed it without finding out whom it belonged to? And the local village bobby knew her bright red little wagon, anyway.

'I'm going in!' As the now familiar Range Rover drew to a halt, Toby disappeared into the house just as it started to rain in earnest. Wonderful. Just wonderful. She turned slowly to face the dark, formidable figure in the driving seat, unaware of the air of weariness that clung to her small frame and the faint smudged shadows under her huge violet-blue eyes.

'Good evening, Miss Murray.' The deep voice was cool and expressionless and as she glanced up into his face she saw nothing that indicated the purpose of his visit. The grey eyes were hooded and distant, the hard features bland. 'I thought I'd better explain about the car.'

'The car?' Whether it was the churning in her stomach that his presence induced or the vague realisation that she hadn't eaten all day she didn't know, but she was suddenly aware of a ridiculous feeling of faintness as she stared into the tough male face. 'My car?'

'Your car.' The cool eyes narrowed as they flicked over her pale face and then he was out of the big vehicle, his touch gentle as he took her arm. 'You look all-in, although I don't suppose you'll thank me for saying so. I think you'd better sit down a minute, and as you've no intention of inviting me into your home...'

He had whisked her up into his arms and deposited her into the seat he had just vacated in the front of the Range Rover before she had time to react or even open her mouth, and now he stood, leaning lazily against the wet vehicle as the rain teemed down on his unprotected head, his eyes mockingly bright as they wandered over her surprised face. 'That's how you should be,' he said indolently. 'Quiet and submissive and incredibly beautiful as befits a little angel. And don't worry——' He put a finger to her lips as she opened her mouth to make an indignant reply. 'I've no intention of getting in there with you. It'd be more than my life was worth.'

'I'm getting down——'

'Sit still, Angel.' It was more the shock of hearing her name spoken by him than the note of cold warning in the deep voice that stilled her limbs and made her sink back into the seat she had been preparing to leave. 'And listen.' He eyed her evenly. 'I've arranged for your car to be repaired—I *said* listen!'

The incensed exclamation that had passed her lips was instantly quelled by the ferocious frown darkening his eyes and again she sank back on the leather seat as she watched the water running in rivulets down his square face. 'I've done that because quite simply I can afford it and you can't and Dr Mitchell is an old friend of mine. It would be inconvenient for him to have to try and work round you managing with buses and lifts and so on, and I can see you *do* need your car.' He glanced towards the house grimly. 'It's a pity you are so out of the way up here.'

'I like it.' She held his eyes defiantly as he turned back to face her.

'I'm sure you do.' A small twist of amusement caught at his mouth for a moment. 'And the fact that I don't approve would be enough to commend it for life, eh?' She stared back at him but made no effort to answer this time.

'Now, the thing was a write-off and is going to take some straightening, but as I didn't imagine you would accept another vehicle from me I decided to get done whatever has to be done, OK?'

'No, it is not OK,' she said weakly. 'I can't possibly let you——'

'If you knew me a little better you would know that "letting me" is not something that ever happens,' he said frostily. 'If I want to do something I do it—understand?'

She held the dark grey gaze as her mind raced, various snippets of gossip that she had heard in her university days coming back to her. An operation that every other heart doctor had said was impossible being performed with impeccable precision and great success. Vitriolic clashes with the 'establishment' that had caused him, at one time, to be ostracised by the more influential members of his profession, a state of affairs which apparently, so the reports had said, had caused him great amusement. Heart surgery in a makeshift theatre after a horrific train crash when a child couldn't be moved, again wildly successful. Of such stories legends were made, and she hadn't believed half of them, but looking at him now…she believed them. Every one.

'But——'

'No buts,' he interrupted her again, his voice becoming milder as he noticed the faintly stunned expression in the tired blue eyes. 'The pound-of-flesh syndrome has its place, but not now. Now you will have to allow me the indulgence of being magnanimous as well as loathsome.'

He moved abruptly, lifting her down from the Range Rover and pushing her towards the house. 'Now just try and leave me with the impression of celestial harmony by not opening your mouth and I'll be in touch in a few days. I've arranged for a

temporary vehicle to be delivered tomorrow
morning about seven by the way, so don't be surprised to see it outside. And one favour——?' He
stopped at the gate and removed his hand from her
arm, for which she was supremely thankful. The
feel of him had burnt through her clothing and the
big body dwarfing hers so completely had felt
altogether...odd.

'Yes?' she asked faintly.

'Keep that brother of yours from any more death-
defying leaps under the wheels of moving vehicles,'
he said drily, 'because if I ever see him do anything
like that again he won't sit down for a week. And
incidentally?' He raised a large capable hand. 'I
was free to kiss you—no wedding-ring.'

She watched him go in numb disbelief, unable to
react when he lifted one hand in a lazy wave as he
turned the big vehicle round and drove off through
the driving rain in the direction in which he had
arrived.

This was crazy, impossible; it wasn't happening... She gazed, like before, down the lane as
she tried to absorb the last few minutes into the
working part of her brain. But it was no good. The
anaesthetising effect of physical and mental
exhaustion held her in its spell until much later
when, after a hot meal and short doze in front of
the fire, she suddenly awoke to the abrupt realisation of what she had allowed. There had been no
more talk of insurance companies being involved;
he had effectively taken the financial burden on to
his own shoulders and, more than that, provided

her with alternative transport while the Mini was being repaired. And he had known it wasn't worth it. She stared helplessly into the flickering red flames as her tired, muddled mind tried to make sense of it all. It would probably cost the earth to repair such an old vehicle.

She gave a long-drawn-out sigh as she continued staring at the fire, which caused Toby, sitting at the table finishing his homework, to glance up enquiringly. In one fell swoop Hunter Ryan had placed her in a hopelessly difficult position. Why had he done it? She rested her chin on her hands thoughtfully. To assist Dr Mitchell, as he had suggested, at the same time as helping her and Toby to retain their independence? That was possible. Unlikely, but possible. Then why did she have the unworthy conviction that after her angry defiance it satisfied something in his male make-up to place her so completely in his debt? The dancing firelight played caressingly over her still features as she gazed pensively into the red glow. And when the time came for the debt to be paid? She shuddered involuntarily as she remembered the big male body and hard face. What then?

CHAPTER THREE

AFTER a surprisingly good night's sleep Angelina awoke the next morning in a calmer and more rational frame of mind. She still didn't understand what had motivated Hunter Ryan to behave so charitably, especially when one considered the day's events as a whole, but he was a rich, attractive and successful man at the peak of a brilliant career. In the cold light of day it seemed the height of vanity to consider that he would bother with her, even for a minute, in the more personal sense. She was a little nobody from the back of beyond, uncultured, unworldly, and he . . . he was anything but. No. She was perfectly safe on that score.

That comforting conviction remained with her until she left the house after breakfast to find a dark, imposing and very regal Mercedes parked at the bottom of the garden gate, the keys of which had been pushed through her letterbox some time since the night before.

'A Mercedes! Oh, wow!' As she shut her eyes for a split-second in repudiation of the beautiful car Toby passed her at forty miles per hour, his young face aglow. 'Look, Angel, a Mercedes!' He danced round the car in a paroxysm of laughing glee. 'You've got to take me to school in it just once . . . please, sis, please.' He raced back to her, snatching the keys from her limp fingers. 'Come on, open it up.'

'This is just a temporary hire car,' she warned him firmly as she slid into the driver's seat after Toby had unlocked the door. 'Until my Mini is fixed.'

'I didn't know they hired Mercedes out like this,' Toby said happily as he sank into the passenger seat beside her, eyes wide. 'I thought you got some beat-up jalopy everyone had used.'

'Hmm...' She glanced at her brother's face thoughtfully. A good point. A very good point. What *exactly* was Hunter Ryan playing at?

After she had familiarised herself with the controls of the car, they returned to the house briefly to pick up packed lunch-boxes, Toby's gym kit and school bag and her handbag complete with shopping list.

'Can I come shopping with you tonight?' Toby asked hopefully.

'You? Come shopping?' Angelina stared at her brother in amazement. 'Since when did you ever want to come shopping with me?'

'Since you got a Mercedes,' Toby said honestly with a cheeky grin. 'Talk about street cred!'

'Street cred or not, I shall do the shopping on my way home as usual,' Angelina said firmly as she ushered him out of the front door and locked it behind them. 'And once you're back you can get the potatoes on, by the way.'

'Potatoes?' Toby looked at her in disgust as he slid into the passenger seat of the waiting car. 'How can you talk about potatoes in a car like this?'

'Very easily,' she answered tartly, 'considering it's me who has to plan the dinners round here.' She glanced at his disgruntled face and relented slightly. 'I'll tell you what, I'll take you to school this morning—just this morning, OK?'

'OK.' Toby beamed at her at once. 'And if I tell you to go slow, go slow, won't you? There'll be somebody I want to see me.'

'Toby, you're impossible.' She smiled at his transparency as the powerful car purred into life at the turn of a key. The Mercedes was a dream to drive and Toby's rapturous delight when several of his classmates did double-takes as they passed just near his school brought a bubble of laughter into her throat.

Once she had dropped him off and begun the return journey to the surgery however, a host of misgivings brought a frown to her eyes. A Mercedes. What on earth had made him arrange for a Mercedes while her Mini was being repaired? Did he expect her to be grateful? *Very* grateful? The frown deepened. She should never have accepted his absurd proposal yesterday. She should have insisted on letting the insurance companies sort it out, even if that would almost certainly mean the loss of transport for good for her. She was being manipulated. She wasn't quite sure how or why, but she was *definitely* being manipulated.

The morning surgery had just finished when the door opened and Shelly's dark head popped round.

The two girls did most of the work on a rota basis, joining together twice a week on the Monday and Friday morning surgeries which were always busy. 'Hi. Can't stop. Just wondered if you're free on Saturday night?' Shelly asked breathlessly from the doorway. 'It's my birthday and Tom has offered to take us all out.'

'All?' Angelina queried carefully. Since working with Shelly she had discovered that the other woman was an incurable matchmaker, and at the moment her target was Angelina. All the unattached men in the district, and beyond, had been paraded in front of her at some time or other, with one or two acutely embarrassing moments.

'You and me and Tom's brother,' Shelly said innocently without batting an eyelid.

'Shelly...' Angelina frowned warningly. 'I've told you—— '

'Oh, I know, I know.' Shelly grinned unashamedly. 'But it'll be a good meal and Martin is at a loose end. No strings attached, I promise. Say you'll come, Angel; you need a break and Toby can stay with my kids. Mum's babysitting. Yes?'

'It's very kind of you——' Angelina began cautiously.

'Great. That's settled, then.' Shelly had disappeared before she could continue what had been going to be a refusal.

Damn! Angelina shut her eyes in exasperation. Shelly couldn't seem to get it through her head that if there was one thing she didn't need at the moment it was the complication of a man in her life. It was all she could do to get through the daily routine most days, and there was the garden to tackle this weekend. Since a certain pair of dark grey eyes had swept in condemning perusal over the weeds and knee-length grass she had flinched every time she left the house.

Still, it was very kind of Shelly to think of her, and a relaxing night out with the other three, all of whom she knew quite well, might be just the tonic she needed. It was unfortunate that Martin had a bit of a 'thing' about her. The frown returned as she considered Tom's younger brother, a good-looking man of twenty-five who, although fun to be with, seemed to have the idea that every female under the age of sixty was helplessly smitten by his charms. But she had made it clear on more than one occasion where he stood and that friendship was all she had to offer, so... She nodded slowly to herself. Yes, she'd go. It couldn't do any harm and it might be fun.

As she walked into the cocktail bar of the exclusive and very expensive country hotel on Saturday night with Martin's hand possessively centred in the small of her back, she was wondering if it would be fun after all. She'd arrived at Shelly's house an hour before with Toby in tow to find an atmosphere of polite hostility reigning. It appeared that Tom's car had broken down the night before and he had spent all day working on it, in the process of which forgetting to give Shelly her card and present that morning and, worse, forgetting to organise the children to do the same. By the time he'd remembered, Shelly had been quietly fuming and dreadfully hurt.

The drive to the hotel, which Tom had insisted be undertaken in his car, had been fraught with long silences and barbed innuendoes, which had seemed to bother Martin not a jot and her a great deal.

'Cocktail, everyone?' Tom forced a bright smile as they sat down. 'Our table's booked for eight so we've plenty of time.'

She was just raising the large conical-shaped glass to her lips in smiling acknowledgement of Tom's toast to his wife, which Shelly had met with her first real smile of the evening, when her heart stopped and then raced on violently at a tremendous rate. Hunter Ryan had just stepped through the door, a tall, sexy redhead hanging on his arm, and was surveying the room with those piercing grey eyes that suddenly fastened on her flushed face and remained there.

'Isn't that...?' Shelly had noticed him too and now her eyes flicked anxiously to Angelina's shocked face. 'It's him, isn't it—that heart specialist chap?'

'Hunter Ryan.' Angelina forced her eyes away from that probing hawk-like gaze with an effort that left her breathless. She couldn't believe the sensations evoked by his presence but somehow, seeing him by surprise like this, the full dominating power of the man had reached out and hit her. The tall, broad body suggested hard, powerful muscles under the beautifully cut suit he was wearing with such ease, his frame more suited to that of an athlete than a surgeon, and, like before, the strong, sensual charisma that was an essential part of him reached out in an arc to draw and subdue. He wasn't exactly handsome, not in the traditional sense, but his attractiveness was electric.

'That's the chap who's lent Angel the Mercedes.' Shelly looked straight at Martin as she spoke.

'Oh, yes?' Martin looked less than thrilled at the development as his gaze landed on Hunter's rugged face before moving to the voluptuous redhead clinging on his arm. 'Bit of a ladies' man, is he?' he asked sourly.

'I've no idea,' Angelina said lightly as her stomach somersaulted uncomfortably. 'This drink is delicious, Tom—thank you.' She smiled at Shelly's husband carefully.

'My pleasure.' Tom opened his mouth to say more but hesitated as a tall dark shadow appeared at his elbow.

'Good evening.' Hunter's voice expressed polite courtesy, nothing else, and as Angelina raised her eyes she saw that he was looking directly at Shelly. 'Angelina.' As the grey gaze switched to her he nodded coolly.

'Hello.' She could hear the breathless tone of her voice and despised herself for it.

'I trust there were no difficulties with the replacement car?' he asked evenly.

'No, it's fine, just fine.' As she spoke she glanced at the woman still attached like a limpet to his side and received something of a jolt as she met a pair of green and very cold narrowed eyes.

'Good. Are you eating here?' As she nodded dazedly he smiled slightly. 'Well, enjoy your meal.' And then he had moved on after including all of them in a neutral nod of his head.

'Wow, he *is* rather gorgeous, Angel!' Shelly was gazing over to where his party of four had seated themselves. 'You've got to admit that.'

'Have I?' Angelina tried an airy smile and took a long gulp of her drink to steady the jangling in her stomach. Disturbing was a better word. And disturbed was how she felt for the rest of the evening. They had hardly walked through into the elegant and hushed restaurant before Hunter's party followed and to her chagrin sat a few tables away, with Hunter directly facing her nervous profile. A turn of the head and she would be looking straight at him, she thought tensely, feeling the cynical eyes burning on her face.

She had dressed carefully for the evening out, her first in months, looping her thick shoulder-length hair into a chic knot on the top of her head which complemented the austere cut of the black silk dress she was wearing and brought the blue of her eyes into startling prominence. She had never placed too much importance on her beauty, absorbing her parents' good solid values at an early age, but now, for the first time in her life, she felt a moment's deep thankfulness that she wasn't plain. Why, she wasn't quite sure. She just felt it.

As the evening progressed and each course came and went she forced herself to act naturally, although each nerve and sinew was vitally aware of the dark figure a few yards away. Each movement he made, every gesture and indication of his head, registered on her senses like liquid fire. She felt sick, confused, caught in a maelstrom of anger and panic that he could make her feel this way just by being in the same room. And he seemed quite oblivious of her presence, laughing and joking with his friends as he ate the excellent food, the odd burst of laughter erupting from their table now and again making her want to clench her hands into a fist.

She glanced over once as they were finishing coffee, and instantly the grey eyes met hers, their expression unfathomable. And then he smiled slowly, something dark and challenging reaching out to her and setting a fluttering pulse racing in her throat, and just for a moment the sensation of being held close to that hard and very male body was as real as though it were happening that minute. Damn him, she thought painfully, damn him. He knew exactly how unsettling she found his presence, and he was thoroughly enjoying every moment of his victory. He was playing with her, like a cruel and satisfied cat with a petrified mouse. But she wasn't a mouse. And she wasn't petrified—not completely.

They sat for some time over coffee and every second Angelina was hoping he would leave, but then, as though fate had joined in the game against her, the two parties rose at the same instant and prepared to leave the restaurant.

'Did you enjoy your meal?' As they walked into the large and thickly carpeted foyer she suddenly realised he was at her side, his face sardonic and cool as he looked down at her.

'Yes, thank you.' As Martin put a possessive hand round her shoulders she saw, just for an instant, a spark of something hot in the grey eyes.

'Good.' He smiled smoothly in farewell as he continued walking with the rest of his party through the foyer and out of the large glass doors into the cold April night, and Angelina saw the redhead slip her arm through his as the shadows claimed them.

'Another drink?' Tom joined them in the foyer after settling the bill and Shelly shook her head in refusal.

'No, let's all have one at our place. You can stay for a while, can't you, Angel?'

'Yes, of course.' She didn't want to, certainly not with Martin in this present mood. He seemed to have totally ignored all her earlier protestations of friendship since setting eyes on Hunter. In fact his attitude had turned distinctly proprietorial, which was ridiculous. Why, oh, why did Shelly feel this need to pair her off with a man?

As they walked out of the hotel and over to Tom's ancient Ford she shivered as the cold night air struck her warm skin and then wished she hadn't as Martin immediately pulled her closer, his hand closing momentarily over one breast in passing. 'Don't,

Martin.' She softened the words with a smile. 'Friends, remember?'

'Friends?' He eyed her leeringly and she realised he was more than a little drunk. 'Come on, Angel, relax a bit,' he whispered coaxingly, his mouth wet.

'I'm quite relaxed, thank you.' Travelling home to Shelly's in the back of Tom's car with Martin was going to be fun, she thought wearily as she climbed into the car, and this was definitely the last time she was ever going to fall in with one of Shelly's 'no strings attached' evenings. If she wanted to be pawed about she'd buy a dog! She glared at him as he moved so far over that he was practically sitting on her lap.

As Tom turned the ignition key there was no response whatsoever from the old car and after a stunned few moments of silence Shelly groaned loudly and vehemently. 'It's gone again, hasn't it— *hasn't it*? Oh, Tom, I could kill you! Angel said we could use the Mercedes.'

'Shut up.' As Tom left the car in one violent movement Angelina shut her eyes weakly. The perfect end to a perfect evening! 'Are you going to help or not, Martin?' Tom enquired after a few taut minutes under the bonnet, and as Martin reluctantly joined his brother Shelly beckoned to Angelina to follow her out of the car.

'I'm going to phone a taxi!' She glared at Tom as she went to walk back into the hotel.

'No way.' He caught hold of her arm angrily. 'It'll cost a fortune and I've already spent the earth on this damn night out. Now just sit in the car and be quiet, woman.'

'Can I be of assistance?' As the cool, silky voice cut into the charged atmosphere Angelina almost groaned out loud. Hunter Ryan. And he must have heard every word.

'I doubt it.' Tom tried to control his voice into more moderate tones. 'Been working on the old girl all day and thought I'd managed to fix her. But I'll soon have her on the road.'

She saw Hunter's mouth twist as Shelly's loud 'huh' of disbelief echoed round the massive car park. 'Well, can I give anyone a lift?' he asked smoothly. 'My friends have just left for London and I saw you seemed to be having a spot of bother.'

'Tom, we could be here all night,' Shelly said angrily. 'Can't we——?'

'Be quiet.' Tom glared so ferociously at his wife that it would have quelled a lesser woman. 'I said I'll fix it.'

'Well, you go, then, Angel.'

Angelina stared at Shelly, convinced her friend had gone mad.

'My kids are tucked up in bed but Toby's waiting for you and Tom could be hours. If Mr Ryan doesn't mind, that is?' Shelly totally ignored her brother-in-law's amazed and furious face as she smiled sweetly into Hunter's dark countenance. As a small warning bell began to ring in the back of Angelina's mind she stared at Shelly in disbelief. No. Not Hunter Ryan. Shelly didn't seriously think there was any chance at all that Hunter Ryan——?

'My pleasure.' Hunter's eyes were purposely veiled as he turned to Angelina and waved his hand to the right. 'If you'd like to follow me...?'

'Look, I don't mind waiting.' Angelina was aware that she was gabbling, but things were happening too fast and although she didn't relish Martin's company the alternative was worse.

'Don't be so silly.' Shelly had that look on her face that told Angelina she meant business. Hunter was the next attempt at matchmaking in her eyes, and no way was she going to miss such a golden opportunity. 'Mr Ryan has said he doesn't mind, and when you collect Toby you can tell Mum we might be late so she won't worry.'

'You could phone her,' Angelina said weakly.

'Go on.' The push was none too gentle and this time Hunter took the decision out of her hands by taking her arm and walking determinedly towards a most magnificent car parked in wicked isolation at the far end of the car park.

'Don't panic, Angel.' His voice was soft and low and more than a little malicious. 'I'm not the Marquis de Sade, whatever you may think.'

'Of course you aren't,' she answered brightly— too brightly—and clenched her teeth in silent protest as he chuckled mockingly at her side.

'You're a tiny little thing, aren't you?' As he opened the door of the Lamborghini she slid into the overwhelmingly luxurious interior with a promise to herself that she wasn't going to be impressed by the car, or him, at all. 'Small and beautiful and quite exquisite.' His voice was deep and soft now as he leant both hands on the top of the car as he peered at her consideringly. 'A lone little angel sent into the big bad world.'

'Very amusing.' She glared up at him determinedly even as her mind registered the fact that he was the most sexy man she had ever met. There was a warmth spreading in her lower stomach that was most alarming, but she couldn't do a thing about her body's reaction to his.

'There's just one thing missing.' He walked round the car after shutting her door, and slid into the driver's seat beside her, which caused her toes to curl into tight knots as the delicious smell of his aftershave sent her nerves racing.

'Which is?' she asked frostily.

'Your wings.' He was laughing at her again, she thought furiously as the grey eyes stroked over her hot face.

'How do you know angels have wings?' she said grimly as she fought for control. It was a ridiculous conversation but she wasn't going to lose her temper, not again.

'Oh, they do.' He nodded solemnly. 'But maybe you're a fallen angel in spite of that air of un-touched virginity?'

She couldn't have heard right, she thought dazedly. He couldn't have just asked her—— No, he couldn't have. 'So this is the famous hundred-and-fifty-thousand-pound car?' she said after a long moment had ticked away in complete silence.

'Adroitly parried, Miss Murray.' He turned in his seat and started the powerful engine, which purred immediately into life. 'Aren't you going to wave to your friends?'

'What?' With a shock of horror she realised they had just passed Shelly and the two men and she had completely forgotten about their existence. Why was she sitting in this car? Why, *why* had she been so criminally stupid as to let herself be manoeuvred into such a dangerous position? And it *was* dangerous. She glanced under her eyelashes at the big dark figure sitting quietly by her side, at the square, hard, masculine face and thick black hair that had a faint trace of silver at the brows. He was an experienced man of the world, confident, assured, with a poise that was formidable. She had never met anyone like him in her life.

'Have I grown horns?'

'What?' As the silky voice spoke lazily into the silence she almost jumped out of her skin.

'You've been staring at me from under those beautiful eyelashes. Are they natural, by the way?'

'Natural?' She stared at him dumbly, quite unable to formulate a coherent reply.

'As I was saying, you've been staring at me from under your eyelashes for a good minute. It's... disconcerting. It makes me want to behave in a way that I thought I'd finished with years ago.'

'It does?' Her end of the conversation wasn't exactly stimulating, she thought faintly.

'It does.' He spared her a brief glance in which she read something that sent fire alarms off all over her body. 'I'd like to stop the car in a quiet spot somewhere and take you there and then.' He

laughed softly and with what sounded like a touch
of embarrassment in the dark depths. 'Not exactly
the way you would expect a senior consultant to
behave.'

'Look, I don't think this was a good idea.' He
frightened her. The self-knowledge caused a fluttering in her chest that constricted her voice. Not
in the usual sense, but in a way... in a way that
touched the very core of her existence and created
a vulnerability, a panic that was as old as time, because there was something inside her that had leapt
to meet the desire evident in that male voice. He
fascinated her, almost hypnotised her, and for the
first time she admitted to herself that she had wondered from the very moment she had laid eyes on
him what it would be like to be made love to by
such a man. Carnal attraction. Pure physical desire.
Animal lust. Yes, it was probably all those things,
but she had never realised before how powerful a
force those *things* were. And she didn't even like
him.

'I've frightened you.' Self-contempt throbbed in
the deep voice. 'I apologise, Angel; I won't hurt
you, believe me.' He glanced at her pale face once
more and swore softly in the darkness. 'The people
I mix with are more worldly-wise, able to take care
of themselves——'

'I can take care of myself!' He'd hit a raw spot
and she was carried along on a powerful surge of
anger that completely washed all thoughts of staying
cool and quiet right out of her mind. 'How on earth

do you think I cope with Toby and the house and everything?' She glared at the dark profile furiously.

'I didn't mean it that way,' he said quickly and placatingly. 'I'm sure you're very efficient——'

'And don't patronise me,' she snapped fiercely. 'Don't you *dare* patronise me, Hunter Ryan. You might be exalted and revered in your own circle and I'm sure you are very good at what you do, but as far as I am concerned you're just a man, with the same bodily functions as the rest of us. The car and your houses and all the rest of it—well, you were lucky, lucky to be born with such a gift as you evidently have.' She took a long, hard pull of air as she ran out of breath. 'And while we are on the subject, you don't frighten me, understand? Not at all!'

'Good.' He had listened to her furious outburst without comment, his face expressionless, and now, as they neared the village, he pulled into a field gateway and cut the engine in one movement. 'Good,' he said again, his voice husky. 'Then I'm going to do what I've been wanting to do all night.'

As he drew her to him she knew she ought to resist, to avoid his mouth as it closed in on hers, but somehow she couldn't. She recognised a thread of sexual curiosity in the dizzy sensation his big body had aroused, a trembling excitement at the unknown; but, more than that, there was an underlying feeling of something else, something hot and fierce and strong, though she didn't dare examine what it was. It had bothered her to see him with that other woman, she acknowledged faintly as he took her mouth in an explorative kiss that caused her nerves to leap in immediate response; she hadn't liked it. She didn't know why; she just hadn't.

His hands reached out to cup the back of her head gently as the pressure of his mouth increased and, as before, a heady sensation of sensual pleasure began to lick through her body in tantalising, fiery waves. He moved slightly, his hands sliding down into the small of her back and his arms drawing her more closely against him so that she could feel the rapid thud of his heart under the silk shirt he was wearing, his suit jacket hanging open. There wasn't the faintest trace of alcohol on his clean, cool breath; he obviously hadn't drunk anything more potent than mineral water, and again she wondered at his almost iron control over himself. Even now, in spite of her inexperience, she could feel that he was restraining his natural ardour, his touch gentle and his hands non-threatening.

'Angel...' As he murmured her name against her lips her stomach contracted at the sensation of her soft breasts pressing against the hard wall of his chest and she found herself wishing there were no clothing between them to impede the feeling that was tormenting her. And that thought, more than any other, had the ability to shock her back into an awareness of the real world.

He had done this all before, hundreds of times before, with many different women; it didn't mean a thing to him. And her? She felt her face burn as she jerked out of his arms, pressing against the side of the car to put some space between them. 'Don't. Please don't.'

'Why?' He leant back lazily in his seat without taking his eyes off her and again she was struck by the sensual animal power he was keeping on a tight rein. He must have women chasing him all the time... The redhead? Why hadn't she thought what the redhead meant?

'Your girlfriend wouldn't like it,' she said shakily.

'My girlfriend?' Sardonic black eyebrows rose over glittering grey eyes. 'Oh, you mean Charlotte, the woman I was with tonight?'

'Of course I mean her,' she said grimly. 'How many women have you got, for goodness' sake?' Now that cold reason was prevailing, she couldn't believe she had allowed him to kiss her like that. Encouraged, almost.

'Well, I don't have them for goodness' sake,' he said with a mocking smile. 'I only like the bad ones.'

She eyed him unsmilingly and he sat up straighter in his seat. 'That was a joke, in case you wondered,' he added smoothly.

'Excuse me if I don't laugh.' She wanted to smooth a tendril of hair from her cheek but knew her hands were shaking so badly that he would notice.

'Charlotte is not my girlfriend.' He stretched his legs lazily as he spoke, his big body clearly uncomfortable in the close confines of the car, and as the material pulled tight for a second over muscled flesh her heart pounded violently. 'She is the wife of a friend of mine, as it happens. The four of them were going to come down for the evening but Gerald got delayed—an emergency.'

'He's a doctor?' she asked uncertainly. At his abrupt nod she relaxed slightly, but only slightly. 'Well, she didn't like me.' As soon as the words had passed her lips she regretted it. What on earth had possessed her to say that?

'Charlotte didn't like you?' he asked in surprise. 'What makes you say that?'

'Oh, nothing, just the way she looked at me,' Angelina said uncomfortably. 'I was probably imagining things. She had no reason to dislike me——'

'She had every reason in the world,' he drawled softly. 'Charlotte is one of those women who likes to have every male eye strictly on her. Did you notice the other woman with us tonight?'

'No.' She shook her head.

'Exactly. That's the way Charlotte likes it. She chooses her women companions very carefully.'

'But I still don't see——'

He stopped her with a wave of his hand, his eyes mocking. 'Do you ever look in the mirror, Angel— I mean *really* look?' he asked quietly. 'You are one of the most beautiful women I have ever seen in my life and Charlotte sensed I wanted you. I do want you, Angel, very much.'

'But——'

'No buts,' he said coolly. 'I know you don't like me—you've made it very plain on more than one occasion—but unless I'm slipping you want me physically nearly as much as I want you.'

'I do not!' Even as she spoke the words she knew they were a lie, and she knew he knew too!

'Little liar...' He moved closer again and she felt hot panic claw at her throat. 'There's just one thing I'm not sure about, or I'd show you how easy it would be. When I touch you, kiss you, you respond so beautifully I can't believe you haven't known a man before, and yet...' he watched the colour surge into her face '...I don't think you have. I, on the other hand, as you so aptly pointed out, have known many women, and after a time one gets jaded—replete.' His face was cynical now, and cold. 'I like your spirit, Angel, and I like your body, but as for anything more, there wouldn't be.' He shrugged powerful shoulders derisively. 'The world, especially my world, has a way of turning love into a four-letter word, and these days I prefer honesty to pillow-talk. Are you following me?'

'You're saying that you don't believe in real love between a man and a woman?' she asked faintly, unable to believe she was actually having this conversation.

'Exactly.' The piercing eyes were watching her very closely. 'And I make sure that my...friendships are conducted with women of the same mind. No complications, no messy emotion. Clean and precise and clear.'

'Like one of your operations?' She suddenly felt furiously, bitterly angry.

'If you like,' he answered quietly.

'No, I don't like.' Something inside was hurting but the anger was paramount. 'I've never heard anything so cold-blooded in my life, if you want to know, and to be absolutely honest I think your world stinks, Mr Ryan, like a putrefying wound that won't heal. You call such liaisons clean and precise?' Her lip curled away from her teeth aggressively. 'Well, I call them cheap and nasty.' Now she really had got through to him, she noted with grim satisfaction as he sat bolt upright, his eyes turning into hard chips of stone. 'Where do all the normal things fit into such thinking? Families, children, a home——'

'And roses round the door?' He eyed her cynically, his mouth thin and tight. 'They don't. They're fine for people who need props like that, but——'

'You don't,' she finished for him flatly. 'Why not?' She almost reached across to touch him in her rage. 'What has happened to you, that you feel this way?'

'Happened to me?' For a moment, a fleeting moment, she saw a stricken expression on his face that was gone the next instant. 'Why does something have to have happened to me? I don't like ties, that's all.'

'I don't believe you.' She saw her words register in the steel-grey eyes. 'You just haven't faced up to whatever went wrong, either because you can't, or because you won't.'

'Really?' Now the control was back, stronger than before, and he allowed himself a lazy, cynical smile as he watched the colour come and go in her white face. 'And all this illuminating psycho-analysis on, what—two, at the most three meetings?' His laugh was cruel and hard and she shrank from it. 'You've missed your vocation, Angel.'

As he started the engine she tried to match his coolness but it was no good. She was shaking helplessly, and as he glanced her way she saw his mouth tighten as he noticed her trembling. 'There's some brandy in the glove compartment,' he said expressionlessly.

'I don't want it.' She felt a dart of rage sweep through her as he shrugged. 'I don't want anything from you, ever. You can arrange for the car to be collected in the morning and have the Mini dumped—anything.'

'Now you are being childish,' he said coldly as he swung on to the main road into the village. 'Are you going to direct me to your friends' house?'

As she gave him the necessary instructions in a small, pained voice she saw that his hands were gripping the steering-wheel so hard that the knuckles were white. He wasn't as in control as he would like her to believe, she thought in surprise. Something she had said, or done, had got through to that razor-sharp mind after all. Or perhaps he was just angry? Angry that she had turned down what he probably considered a very honest proposal? Whatever, she didn't care. She just wanted to collect Toby and put an end to what must be the worst evening of her entire life.

'Just here.' She indicated the house with the Mercedes waiting outside in the street. 'Thank you for the lift.'

'Are you all right to drive?' he asked flatly as she almost fell out of the low-slung car in her effort to escape his presence.

'Of course.' She glared at him through the windscreen.

'Of course,' he echoed with a strange little smile. 'Silly of me to ask.'

And that smile stayed with her all through the drive home with Toby chattering away at her side, through getting ready for bed, and far, far into the night when sleep eluded her. There had been something haunting in his face for that fleeting moment, a hunger, a pain, that she was sure she hadn't imagined.

Stop it, Angel, stop it, she told herself fiercely as the bedside clock ticked another hour away. He was an aggressive, hard, cynical brute of a man; those were the *facts*. All these thoughts and fancies—there was nothing substantial to back them up. She felt attracted to him physically. Well, so what? There would probably be hundreds of men who would affect her like that. It meant nothing, absolutely nothing when coupled with the sort of man he was on the inside. She despised him, loathed him, and if she ever saw him again in the rest of her life it would be too soon.

She pulled a pillow over her head and tried to shut out the pictures in her mind: flashbacks to the restaurant, the journey home, his face ... He had everything he wanted from life; he was happy, satisfied and perfectly content—*he was*. She turned over in the soft bed with an irritable flourish. Of course he was. And he had been right. She had met him on three occasions and they had fought like cat and dog for two of them. How could she possibly know anything at all about him? Well, she could forget him now; they wouldn't have to meet again and she was glad, *glad*. She pulled the pillow tighter and started counting sheep.

CHAPTER FOUR

THE Mini was returned two weeks later with the sort of facelift many an ageing actress would have killed for. Gleaming paintwork, laundered throughout, new tyres... Angelina stared at it for a long time after the cheerful young mechanic had left in the Mercedes. It must have cost Hunter Ryan a small fortune; a new car would have been cheaper. She brushed the exaggeration away irritably. She didn't like this at all, not at all, but she would write a polite letter of thanks, because regardless of his motives it had been a kind gesture, and mention that one day, probably in the far distant future, she *would* pay him back. Every penny. She gritted her teeth determinedly.

She wrote, and rewrote, and rewrote the letter before achieving the light, courteous and civilised effect she was aiming for, and after posting it to his London address she tried, unsuccessfully, to put the whole matter to the back of her mind. She had to get her emotions firmly under control again, she told herself repeatedly over the next few days. The incident was closed, finished with; she would probably never see him again and she was glad. She was. The fact that a certain tall, dark stranger featured heavily in her dreams wasn't her fault; her subconscious seemed to have a life of its own once the iron control she applied during the day was lifted. But she would master that too...eventually.

It was on the sixth day after she had posted the letter, after a particularly trying few hours at the surgery when both patients and doctor had been as awkward as could be, that the irritatingly strident call of the telephone interrupted her evening meal, causing her to jump up from the table with a heartfelt groan as she strode across the room.

'Hello?' The small silence that followed made her aware that her voice had been sharper than she would have liked and she bit her lip tightly before speaking again. 'Hello? This is Angelina Murray— can I help you?'

'Don't say things like that unless you mean them.' The deep, mocking male voice could only belong to one man, and she felt a fluttering shiver down her spine as she recognised the drawling tone. 'And why so cross? You aren't always like this, are you?'

'No.' It didn't occur to her until a few seconds later that she should have pretended not to recognise his voice, but by then it was too late. 'What do you want, Hunter?' She had wanted her voice to sound cool and assured if she ever saw or spoke to him again, but the slightly breathless, husky note fitted neither description.

'Dinner?' The lazy sensuality in the silky voice brought his face in front of her as vividly as though he were in the room. 'Or, to be more precise, I would like to take you out to dinner.'

'Why?' It wasn't a sophisticated response, it wasn't even well-mannered but the word seemed to pop out of her mouth all on its own.

There was another small silence, a little longer this time, and when his voice sounded again she imagined, just for a moment, that there was surprise mingling with the evident amusement in his reply. 'Because I want to see you again,' he said slowly. 'Why else?'

'But I thought——' She stopped abruptly. She had thought he'd washed his hands of her after her very definite repudiation of his advances; she had made it clear that she wasn't in the running for a casual affair after all, but maybe... Her brow wrinkled as her mind raced on. Maybe her reaction had been just the thing that had made him come back for more? He had admitted that he was jaded, world-weary with the women he associated with; a little new blood might be appealing to a man like him. It wouldn't mean anything, not really, but would probably entertain him for a short time until he tired of her like all the rest. How dared he? *How dared he*?

'Yes?' His voice was bland now, almost expressionless.

'I thought I had made it very clear how I felt about you,' she said slowly and firmly after taking a long, hard breath for courage. 'As clear as you made your views on life to me.'

'Ah...' If she hadn't known differently she would almost have thought there was a tenseness in his voice now, but of course that was impossible. He was the most confident, assured individual she had ever met in her life. 'I see.' He paused for a moment. 'It's only dinner I want, Angel.'

She felt her cheeks burn at the casual answer that verged on a snub, but took another deep breath before she spoke. He thought he only had to want something to get it; that was the crux of all this. He wanted her, he had made that much plain, but he was arrogant enough to spell out the terms before he made his move, thinking she would accept them like all the rest. Well, elaborate sexual games weren't her scene; they would never be her scene. If he thought she had been trying to excite him with her refusal, play hard to get, it was time to disillusion him. Once and for all.

'I don't think there's any point, Hunter, do you?' She forced her voice to obey her mind even as her emotions went crazy. 'Your values, your whole slant on life I find repellent and sordid, if you really want to know. You think I'm naïve and childish, I'm sure, but if it's all the same to you that's exactly how I intend to stay. I'm sure you're brilliant at your work——'

'Damn my work!' She was shocked into silence by the raw fury in his voice that had totally replaced the cynical amusement of a few minutes before, but when he next spoke after just a moment the cool control was back with a vengeance. 'A simple "no" would have sufficed, Angel,' he said sardonically. 'It's been a long, long time since I chased a woman——'

'Well, don't start now, then.' She put down the phone before he could reply and then immediately took it off the hook again in case he phoned back. She was trembling so violently that she felt the need to sit down before she fell down, and sank on to the carpet with a shaky sigh. Hearing him, picturing him in her mind had awakened all the dangerous emotions that had been haunting her sleep for nights. Her body wanted him. She shut her eyes in shame at the acknowledgement of her weakness. But her body would have to learn to behave.

'Are you all right, sis?' Toby had finished the fish fingers and chips that he had been eating while engrossed in the TV and now came across to her, his young face troubled. 'What's the matter?'

'Nothing.' She smiled brightly as she put out a hand for him to help her up. 'Long day and difficult people.' And the last one had been the most difficult of the lot, she thought balefully. 'Tomorrow can only be better.'

'Who was that on the phone?' Toby asked curiously as he took in her flushed face.

'No one.' She ruffled his blond hair as she indicated his empty plate. 'No one important, that is. Do you want some ice-cream now?'

'Please.' The promise of his favourite dessert effectively wiped everything else from his mind, and as she ladled a big bowlful of raspberry-ripple ice-cream from the large carton in the ancient freezer she ran her words over again in the tape-recorder of her mind. No one important. And he wasn't. Not now. Not ever.

She had made a promise to herself when her parents died that for the next few years Toby would come first and that she would be both mother and father to him until he was old enough to make his own way. And she would. Part of that commitment meant she had to be here for him to set an example that hopefully would carry him through the teenage years and beyond, when the values he imbibed now would have to sustain him in the real world. And that example didn't include sleeping with Hunter Ryan as a temporary—and, if she knew the man, *very* temporary—appendage to his life, however sexually tempting she found the thought. He was poison, absolute poison, and all the more so because he seemed to be able to touch a deep well of vulnerability she never knew she had. Was it just a dangerous sexual responsiveness to his overwhelming maleness?

She shook her head at her own thoughts. It didn't really matter one way or the other anyway, did it? The decision was made.

The next morning, as she replaced the telephone receiver, the decision taken the night before had cast itself into an iron conviction that was unshakeable. She didn't like the power she had given, albeit unwittingly, to a man who was fundamentally incapable of appreciating sex in anything but its most basest sense. She wasn't the type of woman who could go from man to man and still be happy with herself; she just wasn't. When she committed herself to someone it would be forever; that was just the way she was made and nothing else would do.

Her mind was more at peace than it had been for weeks when the telephone call came through that morning in the surgery. Shelly answered the phone, it being a Friday and their joint rota, and called across to her immediately. 'Angel?'

As she looked up she was conscious of thinking that if it was Hunter the phone was going straight down, when Shelly spoke again. 'It's the school. Toby's ill, I think.'

'Yes?' She had moved across to the desk and taken the receiver out of Shelly's hand before her friend could say any more. 'This is Angelina Murray. What's wrong?'

'Miss Murray?' She recognised the voice immediately as belonging to Craig Hammond, the sports master. 'Now, please don't panic, but there has been some sort of accident.'

'An accident?' she asked faintly as her stomach somersaulted.

'Well, I don't quite know what happened,' he continued quietly. 'One minute Toby was out in front on the cross-country run and the next he was on the ground and gasping for breath. We've had to call an ambulance, Miss Murray.'

'He's that bad?' She tried to keep rational in spite of the mad pounding of her heart. 'Do you think it's asthma?'

'Possibly.' He sounded uncomfortable. 'They are taking him to Raulston Casualty. Shall I meet you there or would you like me to come and pick you up?'

'No, I'll leave now.' There was something screaming at the back of her mind but she couldn't think of it now. 'Thank you, Mr Hammond.'

She left on the run, explaining to Shelly as she made for the car, and as her friend waved her off the whole thing seemed so unreal. Minutes ago her world had been back on course again for the first time in weeks and now... Now something was terribly wrong. She knew it. The thoughts that had surged into her mind during the telephone call came more clearly now. Toby's tiredness, his sudden attacks of exhaustion that seemed to have no rhyme or reason, the faint blue tinge to his lips that she had noticed occasionally. There was something seriously wrong; she should have known, *she should have known*.

Once at the hospital, Craig Hammond met her in the reception area, his young face strained and worried. 'Miss Murray, I don't know what to say,' he said quietly as he walked with her into the main casualty sector. 'They had to give him oxygen in the ambulance, which seemed to help a little.'

'Where is he now?' she asked tensely as her eyes scanned in vain the section which was mainly taken up with somewhat bored-looking individuals sitting staring vacantly into space or drinking lethargically from paper cups.

'In another room.' He gestured uncomfortably. 'They wanted to do some tests.'

'Tests?' Her stomach lurched sickeningly. 'What sort of tests?'

'Look, let me tell someone in authority you're here and then perhaps we can find out something,' he said quickly. 'Have a seat for a moment; I won't be long.'

True to his word, he was back within minutes with a small, thin and severe-looking sister whose grim appearance hid a warm, caring approach that was just what Angelina needed. 'Your brother is in Resuscitation,' she said softly as she sat down by Angelina's side and took her hand gently. 'Now, I understand from his teacher that you are his guardian, Miss Murray. I'm sorry, but could you explain exactly how things are?'

'Yes.' As she spoke about her parents' death and their subsequent circumstances the small woman by her side clucked sympathetically more than once.

'I see.' As she finished the sister rose slowly after patting her hand once more. 'Well, I think it's only fair to tell you that Toby's problem seems to be something to do with his heart. His heartbeat is erratic and fluctuating far more than normal but we won't know properly until various tests are completed. You could see him for just a minute if you like?'

'Yes, please.' Angelina turned to the young sports master and smiled wanly. 'Thank you very much for your help, Mr Hammond; you'd better get back now.'

'I'll stay.' The deep blue eyes in the strong young face looked back at her steadily. 'And the name is Craig.'

'Oh…' She nodded vaguely, all her thoughts with Toby.

Toby was lying with his eyes shut on a narrow bed, his small body connected to various wires and tubes, when she entered the large resuscitation-room at the sister's side a few moments later. She had steeled herself for the worst, but somehow the sight of him stretched out and looking so little and lost in the big room was almost more than she could bear. 'Toby?' She took one limp hand carefully in hers. 'Can you hear me?'

''Lo, sis.' His eyes opened slowly.

'Oh, Toby.' She wanted to gather him in her arms but the tubes and wires monitoring his progress stopped her. 'How do you feel?'

'I'm all right.' He gave a weak version of his normal wicked grin. 'Don't worry.'

'What happened?' she whispered quietly, but he shook his head slightly as his eyes shut tiredly again.

'I can't remember.'

'Perhaps you'd like to wait outside again until we're through?' the sister asked gently. 'I'll call you as soon as you can see him again.'

The next few hours were the worst of Angelina's life. She was conscious of several things standing out from the hazy unreality of it all. Craig Hammond's surprising kindness and concern. Dr Mitchell's phone call to find out what was happening. The little sister's sympathy and understanding. But overall there was a terrible feeling of dark foreboding and panic. There was something dangerously wrong. She knew it. And when the worst was confirmed it was almost something of a relief to have the crucifyingly torturous suspicions dealt with.

'Miss Murray?' It was well past midnight now but Craig Hammond was still with her and she found she was gripping his hand with almost savage intensity as they sat facing the solemn consultant in his office. Craig was a normal, ordinary human being in this sea of starched uniforms and placating voices. 'This has all been a great shock for you.'

'Yes.' She stared at the middle-aged man grimly. Get on with it, she told him silently; just get on with it.

'I'm afraid your brother is a very poorly child,' the impersonal, steady voice went on carefully. 'From the tests we've done to date it would appear that his heart has had some sort of genetic defect from when he was born. Did either of your parents suffer with heart trouble at all?'

'My mother.' She felt as though she was talking from the bottom of a big black well. 'It was discovered after she had Toby; she couldn't work again after that.'

'Quite so.' He nodded several times and then cleared his throat pensively as he met her eyes again. 'Well, as I said, Toby is very ill.'

'Could you explain, please?' She couldn't bear this, she really couldn't. First her parents and now

Toby? 'All of it?' As he did just that and the full
realisation of just how grave things were swept over
her she felt Craig move uncomfortably by her side.
Toby had been given a death sentence. That was
what it amounted to.

'And there is no chance of an operation, anything?' she asked flatly. 'Surely something can be
done?'

'Any operation could only carry the barest chance
of success, Miss Murray,' the consultant said slowly.
'Toby may well live for several years yet with the
necessary medication.'

'And his quality of life?' she asked stiffly. 'What
will he be able to do and not do?'

'Ah, well...' For the first time the consultant
dropped his eyes from hers and stood up abruptly,
walking across to the window in the corner of the
room and looking out over the dark car park below.
'He'll have to be very careful, of course, take things
easy, and——'

'I don't understand this.' She felt Craig pat her
hand as she stared at the man's broad back. 'One
minute I have a normal, healthy brother and the
next——'

'He wasn't healthy, Miss Murray.' The consultant turned to face her, his eyes sympathetic. 'We
just didn't know, that's all. Now, if you——' A
sharp knock at the door interrupted his speech of
condolence and he apologised swiftly before
walking across and opening it himself. 'I said no
interrup—— Good grief! Hunter! What are you
doing here?'

'I've an interest in this case, William.' As she heard Hunter Ryan's calm, deep voice from the corridor outside Angelina rose instinctively and the next minute had pushed past the surprised William and flown straight into Hunter's arms, the storm of weeping that she had been holding in for years suddenly breaking forth in a torrential flood that rendered her blind and deaf to anything but the strong arms holding her so gently.

'Have you any brandy, William?' She heard his voice but couldn't do a thing to respond.

'Brandy?' The other man sounded scandalised. 'But surely——?'

'Have you got any?' The bite in the deep voice obviously had some effect because the next minute something was at her lips and a trickle of burning liquid had run down her throat, causing her to choke and cough helplessly.

'What have you told her?' The sobs were subsiding now but she didn't dare to try and open her eyes. She was obviously still in Hunter's arms, but where the other man and Craig were she had no idea, although she had had the sensation of being moved back into the office. As words flowed and surged over her head she felt herself being pressed carefully into a seat and at that point forced her swollen eyes open.

'OK?' He was kneeling in front of her, his face on a level with hers and the grey eyes more soft than she would ever have dreamt they could be.

'Yes.' She nodded helplessly, her lips still quivering. 'I'm sorry...'

He ignored the apology as though she hadn't spoken and then his eyes switched to Craig, who was standing to one side of the door, clearly totally out of his depth at the new development. 'And you are?' His tone wasn't aggressive, but as he stood up and faced the young teacher she saw Craig flush a little and his shoulders stiffen as though Hunter had said something confrontational.

'I'm Toby's teacher and I was with him when he collapsed,' Craig said stiffly. 'I stayed with Angelina; I didn't want her to be alone.'

'That was very kind of you.' The tone was pleasant enough but Hunter's face had taken on a severity that was distinctly forbidding. 'Very kind indeed, but I'll take care of her now. Can I arrange a lift anywhere for you?'

'Thank you but I have my own car.' Craig turned to her, his face troubled. 'Will you be all right, Angelina? I can stay as long as you need me.'

'No, you go, Craig.' She smiled weakly and held out her hand to him as he moved to her side. 'You were marvellous. I don't know what I'd have done without you.'

'No problem.' He smiled gently. 'I'll give you a ring in the next couple of days if I may?'

'Of course.' She could tell in his eyes that he found Hunter's arrival puzzling but as she felt exactly the same there was no way she could enlighten him as to what it meant. During the long hours when they had waited for news they had chatted about this and that but obviously she hadn't mentioned Hunter at all. Craig must be thinking all sorts of things, she reflected weakly.

'Goodbye, Mr——?'

'Hammond. Craig Hammond.' Craig smiled politely into Hunter's expressionless face and then left quietly after one more nod in her direction.

'Right, William, I'm sorry to burst in like this—a little unorthodox, I know—but Angelina and Toby are old friends.' Angelina looked at Hunter sharply as he voiced the lie but the grey eyes were totally unrepentant as they flickered over her face for an instant. 'Have you any objection to filling me in on the details? I was speaking to Angelina's GP, Roger Mitchell, this evening, who informed me of Toby's collapse, and as I was due to come down tomorrow morning for the weekend...' He smiled coolly. 'You know I bought the Gables a few months ago?'

'Yes.' Clearly Hunter wasn't one of the other man's favourite people but just as clearly he wasn't going to risk offending him either. 'Well, as I see it...'

As she listened to them talk her eyes didn't leave Hunter's face for an instant. Dr Mitchell had called him? Had he asked him to come down here? She couldn't imagine Dr Mitchell doing that, but then everything had gone crazy, desperately, horribly crazy in her world, so why not? Why was he here? Did he think he could do anything for Toby? The sudden rush of hope was so intense as to be painful. Did he?

'Thank you for your co-operation, William.' As Hunter brought the discussion to a close Angelina realised she hadn't heard a word they'd said, but saw that Hunter had Toby's folder under his arm as he stood up, and again the rush of hope was fierce enough to hurt. 'I'll be in touch first thing tomorrow but perhaps we could just look in on the child before we leave. He's in a private room?'

'At the moment.' The other man nodded quickly.

'I'd like him to stay there, please.' Hunter smiled coolly. 'Send any statements to me and just make a note that Miss Murray will be staying at the Gables while Toby is in here, would you? I'll let you know if the situation alters.'

'Certainly, certainly.' As the other man walked with them to Toby's room he was all charm. Clearly her status had risen considerably, Angelina reflected cynically, now that she was linked to the great man himself. But that didn't matter. Nothing mattered. Only Toby.

He was lying fast asleep when they entered the dimly lit room, a young nurse sitting by his side. After a brief consultation with the nurse when he ascertained that there had been no change, Hunter took her arm and moved her from the side of Toby's bed where she had been standing with slow tears dripping down her face again. 'Come on, you're all-in.' He nodded to the nurse as he left, the other man having left them at Toby's door. 'A sedative for you, young lady, and then some sleep.'

She allowed him to lead her out of the hospital, still in something of a dream, but as she saw the lethal red monster of a car some yards away and felt the cool drizzle of the May night on her face she came back to earth with a bump. 'My car's here somewhere...' She glanced about uncertainly. 'But I can't leave Toby anyway; I have to get back——'

He caught her arm as she made to turn and now his voice was brusque. 'He's sedated, Angel, and will be out for the count until noon tomorrow. You need proper sleep, which you certainly won't get in there.'

'Well, I'll go home for a few hours.' She spotted her Mini some fifty yards away. 'Thank you for coming down——'

'You are coming home with me and that's that, Angel.' He stared down at her from his great height, his eyes granite-grey in the darkness and his big body hard and solid under the thick overcoat he was wearing.

'Of course I can't.' In spite of her pain over Toby and the exhaustion that was causing her legs to shake, the old familiar antagonism she felt at his arrogance flared into life again. 'It's very kind of you——'

'Kindness be damned.' He took her arm and almost dragged her over to the waiting car. 'The state you're in, you'll never get home in one piece, and someone needs to keep an eye on you tonight. You've had one hell of a shock.'

'It's not necessary.' She struggled in his grasp but was horrified to feel the tears pricking at the back of her eyes again at his concern. She couldn't cry, not again. She hadn't cried all through the time when her parents had died, or after, but suddenly she didn't seem able to stop. 'It's not, really.'

He swore, softly and very distinctly, as he saw the tears begin to fall again, and then she was in his arms for the second time that evening. 'Stop trying to be brave,' he said softly into the pale silk of her hair. 'Let it all out.'

'I can't.' She jerked away from him as though he had said something obscene.

'No?' He eyed her thoughtfully. 'Angelina Murray, the all-powerful one, is that it? Self-sufficient, needing no one, a law unto herself?'

'You ought to talk.' She stared at him in amazement, furious at his hypocrisy. 'You've just described yourself.'

'Maybe.' The calm, brooding gaze didn't falter. 'But it doesn't come naturally with you, that's the difference. I dare bet you took it all on the chin when your parents died, didn't you? No tears, no outward emotion? You carried Toby as well as yourself.'

'What if I did?' Her small chin jutted out angrily. 'It's nothing to do with you.'

'As a doctor I beg to disagree.' There was something almost cruel in his face now. 'You'll break if you don't use the natural cleansing power of emotion. You've lost your parents and now you've had another crushing blow within eighteen months. The human spirit can only take so much; I've seen it all before. You need to let go, to grieve so that you can face——' He stopped abruptly.

'Face what?' she whispered flatly, her eyes wide with horror. 'Is he going to die?'

'Right at this moment I can't give you any promises, Angel,' he said harshly, raking his hand through his hair in a gesture that spoke of inward frustration. 'I won't lie to you.'

No, he wouldn't lie to her. She closed her eyes for a moment and swayed slightly in her agony. He hadn't lied to her about the way he viewed the female of the species and he wouldn't lie about Toby's chances—but oh, just at this moment she wished he had. He was so cold, so hard, and yet . . . She remembered the sensation of being held in his arms earlier that evening, his gentleness and understanding. But that was the doctor side of him; it meant nothing on a personal level.

'Why did you come here tonight, Hunter?' She was still facing him in the almost deserted car park and now he gestured irritably towards his car.

'Get in,' he said flatly. 'I have absolutely no intention of allowing you to drive home so you may as well concede the point here and now. You're cold and tired and I'm damn hungry, so just get in the car.'

She opened her mouth to argue further but found she was too weary to do battle with the flinty determination in his narrowed eyes. 'As long as you drop me off at my house, then,' she said as she slid into the car after he'd unlocked her door. He didn't answer, merely walking round the car and easing himself into the driving seat with an expressionless face. 'Why did you come, anyway?' she asked again as the beautiful car sprang into life.

'I told you in there—Roger told me about Toby.' He glanced at her briefly as he swung the car in a wide arc and then drove along the quiet road that was part of the hospital premises, joining the main thoroughfare of the country town within moments. 'He'd made enquiries, I understand, and been told enough to think I might be interested in the case.'

'Is that what he said?' she asked quietly as something deep inside flinched. This was just an interesting case to Hunter.

'More or less.' He shrugged casually. 'Does it matter?'

'No.' She shut her eyes as the motion of the car made her light-headed and missed the searching narrowed gaze as it swept fleetingly over her white face. 'It was very good of you to come, though, even if you were coming down for the weekend.'

'I'm a very good man, Angel.' The drawling voice was its normal sardonic and lazy self now. 'Good at a lot of things. I'd love to give you a demonstration of one or two, but now is not the time or the place. How well do you know this young schoolteacher, by the way?' His voice was still lazy and the note of mockery made it seem as though Craig hadn't progressed out of short trousers.

'Craig Hammond?' She settled further into the seat, which was wonderfully comfortable to her tired bones. 'Not very well really; he was marvellous today, though.'

'I wonder why?' he said drily with another swift glance at her beautiful face and closed eyes, the mass of silky golden hair tumbled about her shoulders framing a skin as clear and rich as honey.

'What does that mean?' She opened indignant violet-blue eyes but the hard face was in profile again as he concentrated on the road ahead. 'He was concerned about Toby, of course; he knows him well.'

'Of course.' The silky smooth voice grated on her nerves more than any harshness could have done and she bit her lip angrily before forcing herself to relax again, shutting her eyes determinedly.

'I don't know why you're being sarcastic about him but he was there when I needed him,' she said flatly. 'There *are* kind, generous people in the world, you know, if you look hard enough—even your world.'

'I don't doubt it.' She could hear the mocking smile in his voice even with her eyes shut. 'And there are fairies at the bottom of the garden, of course?'

'You are easily the nastiest man I've ever met,' she said weakly, 'as well as being the most cynical and abrasive.'

'I don't doubt it,' he said again with a dry chuckle.

They drove on in silence for a few minutes, but, now that the conversation had stopped, her anxiety about Toby crowded in fierce and hot again. She wanted to sleep, she would give anything to sleep, but the horror of it all was like a dark, winding tunnel from which there was no escape. Toby, oh, Toby... Her stomach churned and somersaulted violently and she opened haunted eyes to stare out of the window.

'Where are we?' She glanced round in surprise at the unlit road on which they were travelling. 'If you'd kept to the main road there's a lane which leads directly to my cottage. This way you'll come to the village first and have to backtrack.'

'Silly me.' The deep voice was laconic and cool.

'I'm not coming to your house.' She sat bolt upright as his intention became clear. 'I mean it, Hunter.'

She was still arguing twenty minutes later when he turned into the Gables' wide sweeping drive and scrunched to a halt in front of the imposing steps of the Victorian mansion. There were lights burning in several of the rooms downstairs and she glanced at him in surprise as he opened the car door for her, his expression enigmatic. 'I thought you came to the hospital straight from London?'

'So I did.' He eyed her mockingly. 'But there is a little instrument called the telephone which is wonderful for communicating long distance. I called my housekeeper before I left and warned her I might be bringing a guest back and that it could be late. Mrs Jones and her husband normally retire well after one, so I thought they'd still be around.'

'Your housekeeper?' She felt a rush of relief that was transparent as her face and body relaxed. 'She lives in?'

'Of course.' He smiled coolly, well aware of what she had thought. 'I'm sorry to disappoint that fertile little imagination of yours but I'm afraid I have a chaperon to protect me from the more carnal inclinations my body arouses in you.'

It was a heavy dose of self-mockery but if he only knew, she thought silently—he might be nearer the truth than he imagined. It shamed her that, in spite of her desperate worry over Toby, from the moment she had seen Hunter again little prickles of sensation had continued to snake through her limbs non-stop. She had never in her whole life imagined what any man looked like naked, not even her favourites of the big screen, but every time she was with Hunter the thought was there. She constantly had to drag her mind away from the path it seemed intent on following, and found the process intensely humiliating. The only thing that enabled her to keep her head high in his presence was the knowledge that her thoughts were her own, and she had never been more grateful for the fact. He was so big, so dark, so powerful...and dangerous. Definitely dangerous.

'Come along.' He took her arm and at once a thousand nerves sprang into play at his touch. 'Let's get you something to eat and drink and then straight to bed.'

It was said on a purely professional basis, his tone devoid of any dual meaning, but her face flamed in the darkness as they left the car and entered the house. What was the matter with her? What *was* the matter with her? Anyone would think she was a raging nymphomaniac instead of respectable little Angelina Murray with a sensible head on her shoulders and two feet firmly on the ground.

'Angel?' As they stopped just inside the sumptuous hall which was all wood panelling and thick, ankle-deep red carpet, he turned her round to face him and her breathing stopped at the look on his face. 'Welcome to my home.' The subsequent kiss was sweet and deep and she felt herself sinking into it for the few brief seconds it lasted, and then, as the door to the drawing-room opened, she was free. Or was she?

As she said her hellos to the small, plump housekeeper and her equally small, plump husband, she found that her mind was racing in a maelstrom of panic and fear. She was here, in his house. He had arranged Toby's accommodation at the hospital, taken over things with her hardly being aware of it. And maybe, just maybe, he was Toby's only hope for the future, any sort of future. She glanced at the dark, rugged face as he explained the circumstances to the sympathetic housekeeper, who oohed and aahed understandingly.

Somehow, and through no fault of her own that she could see, she had been sucked into this man's orbit like a helpless little speck of debris being pulled relentlessly into the big black hole that would consume it. And she wouldn't be strong enough to withstand him if he still wanted her. She snaked another glance at the austere face. She knew she wouldn't.

CHAPTER FIVE

WHEN Angelina awoke the next morning it was to a room filled with light and sunshine and the rattle of a breakfast tray.

'Good morning, my dear.' The housekeeper smiled at her cheerfully and then plumped up the pillows behind her back as Angelina sat up. 'Did you sleep well?'

'I think I must have done.' She stared back at the little woman in surprise. 'I didn't expect to.' The realisation of why she hadn't expected to sleep had crowded in on her the minute her eyes had opened, and now her eyes moved instinctively to the bedside phone.

'Mr Ryan has already telephoned the hospital, dear.' The small woman had read her mind. 'The little chap is still fast asleep, so I understand, and is expected to remain that way until lunchtime. Now you just relax and eat something—must keep your strength up.'

As the housekeeper bustled from the room Angelina sank back against the pillows, the tray across her lap, and let her gaze wander round the beautiful bedroom. It was the sort of room she had admired many times in glossy magazines while reflecting on the sort of people who had the wealth and influence to support such luxurious living.

Thick white wool carpet, pale peach full-length curtains, with the bedlinen and fitted cupboards in muted shades ranging from deep peach to white. The dressing-table was a dream in pale marble complete with an enormous bowl of fresh flowers whose perfume was scenting the room, and she remembered that the door at one side of the large easy-chair next to the dressing-table hid the magnificent *en-suite*, again in peach and white.

Her stomach churned again as the full enormity of the position she was in washed over her with renewed vigour. She felt slightly light-headed, probably as much due to the sedative Hunter had insisted she have the night before as her empty stomach, and forced her mind to stop racing as she took a determined bite of toast.

He probably wasn't interested in her at all, not after her none too subtle rejection of him a couple of days before, and she had enough to occupy her mind with Toby. Toby's condition had probably interested the professional side of him, awoken his curiosity, after Dr Mitchell's phone call, and equally the doctor part of him had registered her shock and grief the night before and decided she couldn't be left alone. That was all there was to it. The main thing was, could he help Toby? She shut her eyes as a sickening flood of panic took her breath away. He had to, he just had to.

'Good morning.' As her eyes snapped open it was to see Hunter leaning lazily against the open door, his dark face inscrutable. 'I did knock but you seemed to be in a world of your own.'

'That's all right.' She knew the flush that had begun at the tips of her toes had reached her face but there was nothing she could do about it. He looked impossibly dangerous standing there so nonchalantly, his grey eyes almost black in the light, feminine room and his big body clothed in charcoal jeans and matching shirt, the top buttons undone to reveal the beginning of dark, curling body hair. How on earth did his patients react to him? she thought faintly as he walked, panther-like, across the room. He must have women falling in love with him every week!

'Mrs Jones informed me the sedative was a success.' He had flicked the dressing-table stool into one hand as he passed and now seated himself at the side of the bed, crossing one muscled leg over his knee as he surveyed her with those piercingly cool eyes.

'Yes...' Talk, say something, she told herself silently, but it was no good. She had never felt so vulnerable or shy in her life. The housekeeper had provided her with one of her own nighties the night before and, although the length only reached her knees, the bulk of it was loose and voluminous. Nevertheless, she felt like sliding down back under the covers as his eyes wandered over her tousled hair and flushed face and still further, as though trying to probe her body under its layer of cotton.

'You look even better first thing in the morning,' he said slowly after a long, nerve-racking moment, 'in spite of that thing you're wearing. What is it, by the way?'

'One of Mrs Jones's nighties.'

'Poor Mr Jones.' He smiled wickedly. 'But even that looks good on you. Some women——' He stopped abruptly.

'Some women?' she asked quietly.

'Some women don't look so hot in the morning.' There was something almost challenging in his eyes as he stared at her now.

'And I've no doubt at all that you are an authority on that subject,' she said lightly, even as a darting shaft of pain reminded her that she had to keep her distance from this man. He was getting under her skin and she couldn't afford to care about his other women. That would be the height of foolishness.

He didn't answer, leaning back and surveying her through narrowed eyes before indicating the tray on her lap. 'Eat,' he said imperiously. 'I want to see you finish all of that.'

'All of it?' She stared at the loaded tray. Two slices of toast and a small pot of marmalade, a large bowl of fresh grapefruit segments and under a steel cover a plate brimming with sausages, bacon, tomatoes, eggs, fried bread . . . 'I couldn't possibly eat all that.'

'Try,' he suggested laconically as he reached over and poured her a glass of fresh orange juice from the small jug on the tray, placing it in her hand with a small smile. Both the smile and the intoxicatingly sensual whiff of aftershave that reached her nostrils caused her hand to shake slightly as she obediently raised the glass to her lips, and she saw a dark frown crease his brow. 'And try to stop worrying; it won't do any good and Toby needs you calm and confident when he sees you next.'

'I know.' She raised drowning blue eyes to his. 'But I'm so frightened, Hunter.'

'Angel——' He stopped abruptly, raking his hand through his hair in a gesture that was almost angry. 'For crying out loud, don't look at me like that, woman. I'm trying to remember that you're in a state of shock and I've brought you here under my roof for protection, but hell...' He surveyed her through narrowed smoky eyes. 'I'm beginning to wonder if it's me you need protection from. Look, just eat the damn food, will you? We'll discuss Toby later.'

'But——' She bit on her lower lip to stop the tears hovering at the back of her eyes from falling. 'What have I done wrong?'

'Nothing, sweetheart, absolutely nothing.' He had stood up and now leant over her, his control iron-clad again. 'And you need to talk, to let things out, I know that.' He shook his head slightly, his mouth taking on a bitter twist for a second before it mellowed into a rueful smile. 'One hell of a doctor I am.'

'I know you are Toby's only chance,' she said softly, her eyes liquid. 'That other man last night, he was nice enough, but——' She paused, raising her face to his. 'He won't operate, will he, not with the odds so low? No one will. Please help me, Hunter.'

Slowly, very slowly, as though he was being drawn by something outside himself over which he had no control, he bent further and took her half-open mouth with his, his hands moving the tray off the bed as he lowered himself to her side. As his arms closed round her, pulling her against him in a savage gesture of need, she felt herself tense with fright, and then his mouth, his tongue were gentle and persuasive against hers, plundering her inner mouth in delicious darting movements that started a warm, solid ache in her lower stomach and little knife-sharp throbs of sensation in her limbs. As his lips traced a path across one flushed cheek, nibbling at her ear for a second before returning to her mouth, she felt her arms reach up to his neck, his broad shoulders muscled and hard beneath her hands.

His mouth, his hands were subtle and seductive, and although she knew this was a practised technique, that it meant nothing to him beyond the momentary pleasure, she wanted more. After long, slow moments the pressure of his mouth became more intense and then, with a little shock of horror, she realised that somehow he had slipped the nightie from her shoulders, revealing the soft curves of her breasts to his hungry eyes.

Her little moan of repudiation was lost under his mouth and then, as she felt the light stroking movements across her skin, she didn't want him to stop. There was a moist heat filling her now, the alien pleasure that was all so new causing her body to arch and her eyes to open wide in surprise. And he was gazing back at her, the smoky grey eyes hot and fierce as they watched her face.

'Angel, so help me, you know I want you...' His husky whisper caused her to tremble and then, as one hand moved in a slow exotic wander over her back, she shut her eyes tight again. 'Do you understand what I'm saying?'

'Yes.' She couldn't look at him, not when his hands were doing such delicious things to her body. 'Oh, Hunter...' She hardly knew what she was saying as the urgings of her flesh washed over her mind. 'And I know you'll help Toby...'

It wasn't said as a promise for the things to come, nor as justification for allowing the lovemaking to continue; she had meant it merely as a vote of trust, a sureness that he would do the right thing for her brother regardless of what that was; but as his hands and mouth froze she knew he had misinterpreted her whisper. And then he rose in one quick movement and as her eyes opened to meet his she saw that the grey depths were as cold as ice.

'Do you think I'm trying to buy you?' he asked grimly, his face as black as thunder. 'What sort of man do you think I am? I'll do what is right for Toby, Angelina, but the price of your body won't come into it.'

'I didn't mean——'

'I know what you meant.' As he reached across and jerked the material of the nightdress into place, concealing her breasts, she felt as though he had slapped her and shrank from him, her eyes wide with hurt. 'I frighten you, don't I?' he said slowly.

'It's in every line of your beautiful face.' She opened her mouth to deny the accusation, to try and wipe away the furious rage that had turned the hard features to stone, but he turned on his heel in one movement and strode out of the room, banging the door behind him with such ferocity that the walls shook.

She lay there for long seconds, too stunned even to react, and then as the full enormity of the misunderstanding hit her she felt hot tears seep out under her eyelids to form a burning stream down her face, and she turned to bury her face in the pillow and cried as though her heart would break.

'There, there, lovey, I'm sure he'll be all right...' As the warm, comforting voice of the little housekeeper brought her out of the pit of despair she had fallen into, Angelina opened her eyes and sat up, rubbing her face with the back of her hand. 'They can do marvels these days,' the slow Somerset drawl continued, 'and if Mr Ryan has anything to do with it you know you're getting the very best for the little chap.

'Now, you haven't eaten any breakfast and that won't do; it won't do at all.' The small brown eyes surveyed her flushed, tear-stained face reprovingly. 'You go and have a nice shower, dear, and when you come out I'll have a fresh tray waiting for you. Mr Ryan is expecting you to accompany him to the hospital in an hour or two and you can't go on an empty stomach, now, can you?'

As Mrs Jones bustled away Angelina stared after her forlornly. It had been a long time since she was mothered like that—eighteen months in fact—and although she liked being independent and in charge of her life most of the time she still missed her mother acutely. The ache had lessened gradually, but it had taken some time to accept that it was a matter of learning to live with the pain, that she would always grieve for her parents and their un-questioning love.

The tears almost started again but she set her teeth determinedly. She hadn't cried in eighteen months and now she couldn't seem to stop. Well, enough was enough. Toby needed her, there were things to sort out; she couldn't go to pieces now.

And Hunter? Her eyes clouded over and her heart pounded violently. He affected her like no other man she had ever met, and perhaps it was as well he had misunderstood her this morning. She thought of the caresses they had shared and her cheeks burnt hot with a mixture of embarrassment and humiliation. In fact, in the cold light of logic, there was no perhaps about it.

True to her word, Mrs Jones had a tray waiting for her when she emerged from the shower some ten minutes later, hair washed and body glowing. The torrent of warm clean water had done her good, washed away some of the doubts and fears and set her mind on a more stable footing. She would face what she had to face and then get on with making life as comfortable for Toby as she could. All the weeping and wailing in the world wouldn't help and, all things considered, the last thing she needed in her life at the moment was a complication like

Hunter. She *knew* how he felt about the female gender; he had told her himself, after all. She would be the biggest fool on earth to indulge what was merely a strong sexual attraction, and it was criminally unfair to Toby. She needed to keep all her wits about her and be the steady, reliable sister he had always known. She was all he had.

That thought enabled her to eat the breakfast Mrs Jones had cooked before dressing and drying her hair with the small hairdrier she found in the dressing-table. She didn't have any make-up with her but that didn't matter, she thought wryly. The last thing she cared about at the moment was how she looked.

As she walked downstairs a few minutes later she *looked* pretty good to the tall, dark man standing in the hall watching her descend. 'Angel?' He beckoned to her as he saw her falter at his voice. 'A word, please?'

As she followed him into the massive book-lined study she was again conscious of his height and breadth compared to her small feminine curves. He was larger than life in every way, she thought grimly, but she had to be immune to this dangerous attraction; she just had to be.

'I'm sorry about this morning.' He came straight to the point, his eyes remote and severe and his face austere. 'I can only say it won't happen again while you are under my protection; you have my word on it. It was unfair in the extreme.'

'Hunter——' As she spoke his name he shook his head quickly.

'Let me finish, Angelina.' Angelina? Her heart twisted a little. Where had Angel gone? 'I've gone through Toby's notes and had another word with William Herald this morning. I feel it would be advantageous to have some more extensive tests done and I would prefer they be done in London at my hospital. Would you agree with that?'

'Of course.' She nodded eagerly.

'I don't want him moved for a few days yet, until his condition has stabilised, but then we'll transfer him to London and do the necessary. It will probably take a week or so for everything to be done but after that time we should have a rounded picture of exactly how things stand. Now, until we move him I would prefer that you stay here.' As she opened her mouth to object he spoke again quickly. 'I'm going back to London tonight, a dinner engagement, but Mrs Jones will look after you until I return on...say...Friday?' He was watching her very closely but she felt too dazed to notice. 'I assume you would like to be with him while the tests are carried out?'

'Can I?' she asked hesitantly.

'Of course.' He nodded abruptly. 'I've had a word with Dr Mitchell and that presents no problem as far as he is concerned. It is important that Toby is kept as happy and calm as possible, you understand? Now——' He gestured to the door behind her, his face closed and aloof. 'Shall we go?'

'But——' She almost reached out to touch him but something in his expressionless face stopped her. 'It's very kind of you, but I'd rather go home to my own house if you don't mind. There's no need——'

'I do mind and there is every need,' he said coldly. 'Your cottage is extremely isolated, added to which you are going to be spending long hours at the hospital and probably not eating properly. I have one patient to care for; I don't want two. I can contact you easily here and Mrs Jones can deal with the mundane essentials as well as providing company if you feel the need to talk. Now please don't argue with me.' He walked to the door and waved his hand for her to accompany him. 'I shan't be here, if that's what's troubling you,' he said icily. 'Now, let's get to the hospital.'

His attitude set the tone for the rest of the day, at least with her. She noticed that once they were with Toby he unfroze completely, exchanging a careless banter with the boy that indicated an ease with children she hadn't suspected. By the time he left the room an hour later it was clear that Toby had developed a severe case of hero-worship.

'Isn't he great, sis?' Toby's face was a more normal colour today, she noted thankfully, although the blue tinge to his lips hadn't completely cleared. 'Did you hear him say I could drive his car when I'm better? He's got a huge field attached to his house and he says I can go round that with him.'

'Mmm . . .' She nodded carefully. 'How do you feel, then?'

By the time Hunter returned to collect her at six o'clock she felt as tired as though she had run a marathon. Toby had drifted off to sleep watching his favourite TV programme and as Hunter's dark head appeared round the door she rose quietly, switching off the television as she passed after dropping a light kiss on Toby's head.

She glanced at him under her eyelashes as they walked down the long corridor, and her heart lurched for a moment before resuming its steady beat. He was dressed in a dark dinner-suit and snowy white shirt, every inch the rich, remote consultant who had the world at his feet, his dark hair with its slight touch of silver swept back and his face hard and uncomprisingly severe.

'Who are you having dinner with?' She had fought against asking the question and lost.

'A friend.' The reply was abrupt.

'Male or female?' she asked lightly. It was stupid, really stupid because she knew the answer anyway.

'Does it matter?' He glanced at her coolly as they reached the car park. 'I called in and picked up the things you asked for, by the way.' He indicated a suitcase in the back of the car. 'Here are your keys.'

'Thank you.' As their fingers touched for a brief moment she felt the shock of it in every pore and nerve of her body.

The drive back to his house was conducted in total silence and she realised, as she glanced at the hard profile once or twice, that he really had drawn away from her. The remote face, relaxed body and undeniable air of coldness was real. Whereas she… She bit her lip angrily. She was a mess.

'Goodnight, Angelina.' He escorted her to his front door and after opening it turned to leave.

'Aren't you coming in?' she asked in surprise before she could stop herself.

'No. My dinner engagement is for eight o'clock,' he said calmly. 'Mrs Jones has prepared a light supper for you which you can have in your room if you prefer. She will bring breakfast at nine tomorrow so try to sleep in a little. Your car is in one of the garages, incidentally.'

'Is it?' She stared at him, her eyes wide.

'The key was on the keyring you gave me this morning so it seemed logical to get it here for you for the morning.'

'And you are a very logical person, of course.' She didn't know what little devil prompted her to provoke him but the cool, untouchable air was incredibly galling. In fact he was the most infuriating man all round. Here he was, providing food and shelter and taking Toby into his care at the same time as almost ignoring her and going off to have dinner with another woman. And he was perfectly within his rights to do so. That was what made it even harder to take.

'Usually.' As the cool grey eyes moved over her angry face his mouth hardened. 'You would have preferred me to leave the car in the hospital car park? Is that it?'

'Of course not,' she said sharply.

'Then stop being so childish.' He was halfway down the steps when she spoke again, and this time her voice was muted and low.

'You make me *feel* childish when you treat me as though I'm Toby's age. I'm a grown woman, Hunter, not——'

'I know what you are.' He swung round so violently that she almost stepped backwards before she controlled the impulse, watching him with wide eyes as he returned to her side, his face dark and angry. 'Dammit, woman, what exactly do you want from me anyway? Is it this?'

This time his arms were hard and ruthless as they held her to him in an embrace that had no tenderness in its depths, just wild, brutish rage, and his mouth seared the soft flesh of her lips as he ground them apart to take her inner mouth in a harsh, cruel kiss that was meant to punish. She struggled at first, wildly, and then became still as she realised that her small frame was no match for his superior male strength. It was only seconds before she was free again as he thrust her from him with a small groan, his breathing thick and ragged.

'Damn you, Angel.' He stared at her in the scented dusk. 'That's the first time I've broken my word since I was a boy.'

She stood, her hand to her bruised mouth, as he strode savagely down the steps and over to the menacing Lamborghini waiting silently on the drive, her thoughts frozen and her mind numb. The car screamed a circle on the pebbled drive, roaring away as though to prove its boast of being able to reach a hundred miles per hour in twenty seconds, and then was gone in a whirl of red metal, the sound of its engine dying on the thick air as the startled

squawks from a family of crows nesting in one of
the massive old trees bordering the drive filled the
shattered evening with protest. The heady perfume
of lilac drifted on the cool evening air from several
bushes near by, the faint tang of woodsmoke mixed
with wallflowers was there too in the dusky stillness,
but, although the old familiar smells she had grown
up with normally comforted and soothed, tonight
they merely added a poignancy to the evening which
was unbearable.

Angelina breathed deeply, her hands wrapped
round her middle, and shut her eyes to blot out her
thoughts. She should have *thanked* him for bringing
the car back; what had she been thinking of? And
allowing her to stay here, and Toby... How could
she have been so ungrateful, so unappreciative of
all he was doing?

Because you didn't want him to spend time with
another woman? her mind asked quietly.

'No.' She spoke out loud into the empty night.
Of course that wasn't it; it wasn't. She shouldn't
have provoked him the way she had, especially after
all he'd done, but—— Her mind stopped abruptly.
She wouldn't think of all this now, anyway; she
was too tired and it wouldn't do any good.

Who are you fooling? that little voice in her mind
asked again, but she turned swiftly and opened the
front door of Hunter's house, stepping into the
wide, elegant hall as though she was escaping from
something. He had gone to London to spend some
time with one of his women. Fine. Absolutely fine.
There was no reason in the world why he shouldn't.

CHAPTER SIX

THE next few days were difficult but by the time
Hunter was due to return on Friday Angelina felt
that overall they had passed relatively smoothly.
Time dragged at the hospital but she was there at
ten o'clock every morning and didn't leave until
after dusk, playing board games with Toby, reading
to him when he was too tired to concentrate himself
and generally just trying to make his days less uncomfortable. Craig Hammond popped in for an
hour or so after school every day and she found
herself looking forward to his visits. She could relax
in his company, even dozing off once or twice while
he was entertaining Toby if the day had been
strenuous, and the uncomplicated warmth of his
friendship was wonderfully soothing on her shattered nerves.

The three of them were laughing at a TV programme on Friday evening, Craig's long body
perched precariously at the end of Toby's bed close
to her big easy-chair, when a sharp knock at the
door followed by the immediate entry of a grim
Hunter cut the laughter dead.

'Good evening.' He nodded dismissively at Craig,
the grey eyes narrowed and cold, and as his gaze
moved to Angelina they iced over still more before
he turned to Toby, who was sitting up in the bed

looking eagerly at his hero. 'And how are you, young man?' he asked quietly, a warmth in his face that had been totally absent with the adults.

'Great.' Toby grinned back. 'Angel says I'm going to move to your hospital soon, Mr Ryan.'

'I think in view of the fact that we are going to be seeing a great deal of each other over the next few weeks it might be as well to drop the "Mr Ryan", don't you?' Hunter smiled into the too pale young face as his professional gaze noted the pallor. 'Hunter will do fine. And we're going to transfer you this weekend, if your sister is happy with that?' He turned to Angelina again, dark brows raised enquiringly.

'Yes, of course, anything you say.' She saw the sardonic gleam in the grey eyes at her obedient reply but didn't rise to the bait, forcing a cool smile on her lips as she held his gaze. 'You're the doctor.'

'Indeed I am.' The grey eyes switched back to Toby. 'And with that in mind I think that my patient has probably had enough excitement for one day. I'd like to give Toby a quick examination, so perhaps if you wouldn't mind...?' He indicated the door with a lazy wave of his hand. 'You're in your car, of course, Angel?' he asked smoothly.

'Yes.' He would have seen it in the car park, she thought quietly; there had been no need to ask.

'Then I'll meet you back at home.' It was a simple sentence and said with an air of innocent intimacy that was a clear message to the other man sitting watching them, but, rising as she was to collect her handbag and coat, Angelina missed the real import of his words, which only registered on the way home and caused her to grind her teeth in impotent rage.

'I'll meet you back at home.' It sounded as though... As though she were his mistress or something. She remembered Craig's somewhat cool goodbye in the car park and drew the breath in through her mouth in an angry hiss. Hunter had done that on purpose: set out to give Craig the impression that they were more than—— More than what? She wrinkled her brow wearily. What were they exactly? Hardly *good* friends, not even friends in the real sense, but not anything else either.

She felt the throb of pain she had been fighting against all week take hold of her senses once more. She didn't understand him; she really didn't. He had cold-bloodedly warned her that any liaison with him would be short and for one purpose only—which apart from its lack of romance was hardly an aphrodisiac to anyone normal—as well as cautioning her that he wanted no commitment, no involvement, no ties in any way in his life. And then—she shook her head at the inconsistency—then he had virtually carried her over the last week when she had needed someone as never before in her life, providing financial support, a roof over her head, and the capable Mrs Jones to take care of all her immediate domestic chores like cooking, washing clothes and so on.

Why had he done all that? Was Toby's case so very interesting, so unusual? But perhaps it just presented him with another of those hundred-to-one challenges that he was so good at meeting. He had said he was jaded and world-weary; maybe that applied to his work too?

She had only been back at the Gables for a few minutes and had just kicked off her shoes in her bedroom, preparatory to taking a long, cool shower to wash away the antiseptic odour that hung to her clothes and hair from the hospital, when Mrs Jones called before knocking on the door and popping her head in the room like a bright-eyed robin. 'Mr Ryan telephoned earlier—did you see him?' she asked cheerfully, her head bobbing in agreement with Angelina's nod. 'Well, he wants dinner ready for eight-thirty if that's all right, dear? In the dining-room, of course. That'll leave you plenty of time to get ready, won't it—it's only seven now?'

'Yes, that's fine, Mrs Jones, thank you.' Angelina smiled quietly, her heart pounding at the thought of a meal for two.

Once alone again, she stripped off her sticky clothes gratefully—the hospital's central heating was always far too high—and padded through to the bathroom, washing her hair and luxuriating under the shower for long, lazy minutes. The warm water was wonderfully soothing on her overheated body and tired limbs, its caressing, gentle flow more therapeutic than any massage, and she stretched slowly like a small cat. She had just wrapped a hand-towel round her wet hair turban-fashion and swathed her body in a thick, fleecy bath-sheet when a knock at the outer door wrinkled her brow. Mrs Jones again? What now?

'Just a minute.' She was halfway across the room when the knock sounded again, angry and sharp, and this time she paused uncertainly. That wasn't Mrs Jones at the door.

'Angel?' Hunter's voice was throbbing with impatience. 'Can I have a word with you?'

'Could it wait until dinner?' she asked warily as she pulled the soft towelling more securely round her damp body.

'Not really.' He sounded angry and harassed, his tone abrasive. 'I want to talk to you *now*.' The authoritative ring brought hot, indignant colour into her face, and she took a steadying breath as she bit back the tart reply hovering on her lips. This constant conflict was doing neither of them any good; someone had to give a little.

'OK.' She adjusted the towel still closer to her body. 'I've just had a shower, but——'

He had opened the door while she was still speaking and immediately her pulses leapt at the sight of him, big and dark, in the doorway. 'Oh...' Was that a flare of colour under those hard, masculine cheekbones? she thought in disbelief as his eyes took in the sight of her, small and still, standing in the middle of the beautiful room. 'I didn't realise you weren't dressed; shall I come back later?' he asked abruptly.

'No, it's all right.' She tried a tentative smile but there was no answering warmth in the harsh face. 'Will it take long?'

'I doubt it.' He eyed her grimly. 'Do you think it wise to allow free access to every Tom, Dick and

Harry into Toby's room? He needs rest and quiet at the moment. I thought you understood that.'

'I do.' She stared at him indignantly. 'He's had very few visitors, just a brief visit by Dr Mitchell and Shelly one night after work and Craig brought his best friend round to see him on Wednesday. That's all.'

'Not quite.' He took a step into the room, shutting the door behind him. 'Toby tells me Craig Hammond has been to see him every night.'

'Oh, Craig...' She nodded quickly. 'Of course Craig's popped in. For some reason he feels responsible for Toby's collapse, as it happened when he was stretching the lads in cross-country to see who would compete in the area sports——'

'I'm not interested in all that.' He cut off her voice with a harsh movement of his hand. 'If tonight was anything to go by, Mr Hammond has no idea at all how to conduct himself in the presence of a sick child.'

'Well, that's just ridiculous!' She stared at him in utter amazement. 'Craig's been wonderful, keeping Toby entertained while I pop out for a coffee and a break and bringing messages and cards from all his friends. We've really appreciated——'

'Ah, now we get to the crux of the matter,' he countered acidly. 'By "we" I guess we can substitute "I"? Well, I'm sorry, Angelina, but you'll have to do your courting elsewhere.'

'How *dare* you?' For a split-second she couldn't believe she had heard right, but now, as the colour flamed in her cheeks and her eyes spat sparks, she

had an overwhelming urge to hit him. 'How dare
you say that to me?'

'Quite easily.' He folded his arms as his eyes narrowed into grey slits, his muscled legs slightly apart
and his whole stance one of extreme arrogance.
'Toby is my first concern.'

'And mine!' She knew her voice was too high
but there was nothing she could do about it. It was
taking all her control not to leap on him and
pummel her fists against that superior, mocking
face. 'Craig is one of Toby's teachers, nothing
more.'

'Now it's you who's being ridiculous,' he said
icily. 'Do you seriously expect me to believe that
you don't know how the guy feels about you? He's
crazy about you, Angelina; it's in every look, every
gesture he makes.'

'I don't believe that, but even if it was true that
doesn't mean to say I've either encouraged him or
that I feel the same, does it?' she asked hotly. 'You
can't tell me you haven't reached the age of—
what . . . ?'

'Thirty-nine,' he put in coldly.

'Thirty-nine, without someone fancying you
when the emotion wasn't returned? Well, can you?'
She glared at him furiously. 'Besides which, Craig
is only twenty-four and hasn't bothered much with
girlfriends from what I understand. He's crazy
about sport——'

'Twenty-four?' he said tightly. 'What are you
trying to say—that he is more your age than I am?'

'What?' He was talking in riddles, she thought angrily. Were they having the same conversation or what?

'Because, if you are, I can assure you of one thing,' he continued tautly, his body as tense as though he was going to pounce any moment. 'He would bore you stiff within weeks.'

'Craig?' She shook her head bewilderedly, trying to make sense of the way things were going. 'But it's never been mentioned that I go out with Craig——'

'It will be,' he said coldly. 'Believe me, he won't wait forever. And what will your answer be if he does ask you out?'

Just for a second she was tempted to tell him and then pride came to her rescue. He had made it clear, crystal-clear, that as far as he was concerned she was just a female like all the rest and good for one thing only. Well, so be it. But there were other men who found her attractive for more than merely what her body could offer. And it wouldn't hurt him to acknowledge that.

'I rather think that's up to me, don't you?' she said tightly. 'If and when the situation occurs.'

For a moment he continued staring at her and then dark rage transformed the hard, cynical features into something frightening as he swore softly under his breath, his arms unfolding and his hands reaching out to hold her in a bruising grip. 'Don't play with me, Angelina,' he said with soft, menacing control. 'You're on dangerous territory.' He shook her slightly as he spoke and the movement dislodged the towel from her head, golden silky waves falling in tumbling disorder about her face and shoulders. 'I could have you begging me to take you within two minutes, you know that. You might not like it, but you know it. Does he excite you like that? Does he?'

'Stop this.' She didn't dare to struggle; the towel wrapped around her body was in dire straits anyway.

'Then answer me.' His eyes were glittering with a brilliant fierceness but the rest of his face was as cold as ice. 'Do you want him?'

And it was in that moment, for no clear reason that she could explain either at the time or afterwards, that she knew she had fallen in love with Hunter Ryan. There was no logic in it, not a shred of common sense, but she knew it with a certainty that doused her anger with sickening pain and panic in the same second as her mind told her she had to keep the revelation from him at all costs. She had to remain cool. 'Let go of me, Hunter,' she said carefully. 'You gave me your word that I would be safe under your roof. My relationship with Craig is nothing to do with you any more than yours with the woman you went to see last weekend is to do with me.' Let go of me, her mind was screaming; let go of me before you read something I don't want you to. I can't let you guess how I feel, not now, not ever. 'I *have* taken care of Toby this week, whether you accept that or not. He is my only priority at the moment, I can give you my word on that.'

'And that's an answer?'

As he let go of her, pushing her from him with a savage gesture of repudiation, she felt the towel slip from her body and fall to the floor before she could save it, and as the dark grey eyes flashed over her nakedness she knew total and utter humiliation. And then he moved swiftly, flicking the bathsheet round her more quickly than she could have done, his face rent with such a mixture of emotions that she could hardly pick out one, though she saw hunger there as well as a dark self-disgust that rent her soul.

'I'm sorry, Angel, that wasn't planned, believe me.' He hugged her to him for one second but even in that short moment she felt the arousal his body couldn't hide, and then he had gone, striding across the room in two savage steps and out through the door without a backward glance. As it shut behind him she sank on to the thick carpet with her mind and body frozen. She had to get away from here, anywhere, now...

She hung her head down over her chest, her eyes closed. She shivered suddenly as she remembered how her arms had wanted to hold him close, reach out to him... Why hadn't her brain told her that this feeling that had consumed her almost from the first moment of seeing him had been more than just physical desire? She should have had some deep-rooted feminine instinct, some primitive awareness to let her know before it had had the chance to grow, to flower... And now it was too late, much too late. She couldn't leave, there was nowhere to go, and, besides, Toby needed her. She groaned softly as she rose from the carpet and walked to sit at the dressing-table, looking at her pale reflection with drowning eyes.

She loved him. Her heart pounded even as the blood in her veins turned to liquid ice. She loved a man who had no belief in such a concept. And for the next few weeks, months even, she was going to have to endure seeing him every day, knowing that he held Toby's future in his hands, those large, capable, masculine hands that could work such apparent miracles on the operating table. And whether Toby lived or died—her heart thudded again savagely—she would go on loving him and every day would have to keep the knowledge from him. Because if he ever guessed . . . her eyes opened wide with despair . . . it would lead to his bed. But only his bed. Because he wanted her; physically he wanted her very much. *But only physically*. There would maybe be tenderness involved, certainly pleasure and carnal satisfaction, but overall she would just be another in a long line that meant very little. He had told her. *He had told her*.

It took all the courage she possessed to walk down to dinner as though nothing had happened. She dressed carefully in a plain black dress that fell in full, swirling pleats almost to her ankles and had long sleeves and a high neck. She wanted to hide every inch of her body from his gaze tonight just as she had to hide her soul. She left her hair free to form a shining veil and used the minimum of make-up and in consequence looked more ethereally beautiful than she had ever done before, although she was totally unaware of it.

Hunter's face was dark and tense when she joined him in the dining-room on the dot of eight-thirty, and as he rose and pulled out her chair, standing behind her while she was seated, the cold grey eyes closed momentarily as though the sight of her hurt.

'Angel——' As he spoke she raised her hand quickly, nervous exhaustion making her voice high.

'Please don't say anything,' she said shrilly. 'Not about what happened upstairs.' She took a deep breath as he seated himself opposite, looking at her over a table glittering with exquisitely worked silver cutlery and fine glasses. 'It was a mistake, we both know that; let's just forget it.'

'Can you?' he asked grimly. 'Forget it?'

'Yes.' She forced her eyes to meet his and betray none of the stark anguish that had her stomach clenched in a giant knot. 'If you can. You're doing so much for Toby and me and I'm very grateful.' She carried on quickly as the hard face darkened. 'You might not like me to say it, but I am. You misunderstood things tonight and we've cleared the air; let's leave it at that. But there's one thing.' She had to say it, she told herself painfully; it was her only protection for the future, for any sort of safety from her own wayward desire and traitorous heart. 'Yes?'

'After you left my room I sat and thought—examined my heart, if you like.' He sat up very straight and there was a strange look to his face that almost froze the words—almost. 'And I decided that, although I hadn't thought about it before, I do like Craig Hammond, quite a lot.' She dropped her eyes as though in shyness but mainly because she couldn't continue looking at him and lie. 'So, although I wouldn't do anything about it before Toby's well, afterwards...' She let her voice trail away slowly.

'I see.' She didn't dare glance upwards; the very air around them seemed to be thick with a menacing heaviness that was making her breath come in short, hard gasps.

'I thought I'd better just set the record straight,' she continued painfully. 'It's only fair.'

'Only fair. Yes, quite.'

He wasn't making this any easier, she thought sickly. Did the possession of her body really mean so much to him? But then forbidden fruit was always the most tempting, even if once one had sampled it it was relegated to the dustbin like everything else. She raised her eyes slowly, expecting she knew not what, but the rugged male face in front of her was set in a remote mask, his eyes distant and cool and his mouth straight.

'You see, I'm not like you or the women you usually like,' she said quietly, her eyes shadowed. In this, at least, she could tell the truth. 'I couldn't go from one man to another; I'm just not built like that. I know you think it's naïve, impossible even, but when I give myself to someone it will have to be forever. I want children, a home...'

'Roses around the door?' he said flatly.

'Yes.' Her eyes were defiant now. 'That too.'

'And you think Craig Hammond will provide all that?' he asked grimly.

'Maybe.' She lowered her gaze again as she fiddled with a silver fork. And maybe not, her mind said silently. She couldn't let herself think yet about the long, barren years ahead when she would be alone. And she *would* be alone. She wouldn't settle for second best; no one but Hunter would do. There would be no children, no husband to share with, laugh with, grow old with. He had ruined it all. But maybe, if he could save Toby, then all the pain would be worthwhile in the end? She bit her lip hard before glancing up as Mrs Jones bustled into the room with the first course—two steaming bowls of home-made beef soup.

How was she going to eat? she asked herself silently as the smell of food made her want to heave. But she had to. She had to appear normal and calm and composed; it was the only way she was going to bring this whole charade off, and he *mustn't* guess how she felt—he mustn't ever guess. She couldn't bear it.

Eventually the subtle torture ended. Once back in her room, Angelina sank down on to the bed weakly, her eyes blank. During dinner Hunter had informed her, in a tight, cold voice, that they were leaving first thing in the morning for London.

'So soon?' She had raised surprised eyes to his severe countenance. 'But I thought——'

'You would have time to make some farewells?' he'd asked flatly. 'Only by telephone, and then only if you must. We shan't have a great deal of time

in the morning. I want Toby to be established in
the hospital by lunchtime at the latest.'

'I see.' She'd glanced at him nervously. 'Do I
follow by car or——?'

'You can make the journey with Toby in the ambulance or ride with me,' he'd said coolly. 'Obviously Toby would like you to be with him.'

'Yes.' She'd nodded quickly. Because you clearly
wouldn't want me to be with you, she'd thought
bleakly.

As she glanced round the beautiful room her gaze
fell on the telephone at the side of the bed.
Normally it was left unplugged, Mrs Jones taking
all the calls from the phone downstairs, but each
bedroom had its own phone and extension plug for
any outside call that might be required. She hadn't
used hers yet, although Hunter had indicated that
she was quite free to do so, and now she slipped
the tiny plug into its socket and dialled Dr Mitchell's
number. She needed to talk to someone, anyone,
besides which he had asked to be kept informed on
the move.

'Braybrook four five nine.' As the older man's
firm, calm voice came on the line it felt like a touch
of sanity in a crazy world. 'Dr Mitchell speaking.'

'It's me—Angel.' She took a deep breath; that
ridiculous urge to burst into tears was back again.
'I thought I'd better let you know we're leaving for
London tomorrow morning, so it might be another
week before I'm back at the surgery.'

'I told you, Angel, you take as long as you like. Your job is perfectly safe until you return; Toby is your only concern, and rightly so. How is he?'

'A little stronger, that's all,' she said slowly. 'Hunter is anxious to get on with the tests now, I think, to find out what's what.'

'I can understand that.' There was a brief silence and then Dr Mitchell spoke again, his voice faintly curious. 'I was surprised he came down to the hospital like that, Angel.'

'The hospital?' For a brief moment she thought he was referring to Hunter's cavalier treatment of Craig that night and her brow wrinkled in confusion. How did he know?

'Last week, when Toby collapsed,' Dr Mitchell said impatiently. 'It was most strange altogether, really. He called to ask if your car was behaving itself after the accident but I got the impression there was something more, something he was finding it difficult to ask. And when I mentioned Toby's illness he got quite irate that I hadn't more facts to give him.'

'Did he?' she asked faintly. But Hunter had given her the impression that Dr Mitchell had phoned him thinking he would be interested in the case, hadn't he? Yes, he had. She was sure he had.

'At that stage the hospital wasn't even sure if it was Toby's heart causing the problems,' Dr Mitchell continued quietly, 'at least from what they told me when I telephoned. So I phoned Raulston General back again and got a little more information, but when I tried to phone Hunter at his London number he'd already left, presumably to see Toby, because I understand he was with you a couple of hours later.'

'Oh, I see.' She sat back on the bed, trying to digest what her ears had heard.

'I suppose Hunter felt an interest in the boy after almost running into him,' Dr Mitchell said thoughtfully. 'I understand he was a little severe with Toby at the time?'

'Yes.' She nodded to the phone and herself. That was it. He'd felt obligated in some way—guilty even, perhaps? That had to be it.

It was almost three when her eyes closed in sleep and she awoke with the birds, rising from her bed to survey the pale grey morning from the bedroom window, her face white and her eyes shadowed. The next few days would ascertain if any sort of operation was possible or not, and also Toby's chance of survival. She felt a pain in her hands and looked down to see that her fists were clenched so tightly that her fingernails had drawn blood on the palms of her hands.

She had never felt so frightened or confused or desperately unhappy in all her life, not even when her parents died and she had left university to cope with a small and painfully disturbed young brother as well as the loss of the two people dearest to her in all the world, and the cessation of all her student dreams. But, despite the overwhelming heartache of that time, the bitter questioning and long, sleepless nights, she had still had some hope for the future. But now...

She watched a tiny pair of robins in the ancient copper-beech tree opposite her window emerge from the glowing red leaves and fly down to search for titbits in the moist earth below, returning almost immediately with fat insects in their beaks and then swooping down again, their bright black eyes eager. They must have a nest hidden in the thick branches, she thought bleakly—a nest with little ones.

And that was *normal*. Suddenly all nature seemed to mock her. Insects, animals, humans...they all found a mate, procreated; it was part of life's cycle, a natural progression that kept the world in balance. And now she was going to have to take a solitary path. Suddenly fierce anger replaced the bitter misery of the long night hours. It wasn't fair; this just wasn't fair.

She was hoping Hunter wouldn't be in the breakfast-room when she went down some time later, but as she opened the big, beautifully carved oak door her stomach lurched as her eyes took in the figure sitting at the end of the pine breakfast-table, partially hidden behind an open newspaper.

'Good morning.' He glanced up briefly, his face straight, and she nodded a reply before helping herself to a cup of coffee and a slice of toast, seating herself at the other end of the table and forcing herself to begin to spread some apricot preserve on the toast as though this were just a normal day. 'Did you sleep well?'

'Not particularly,' she said quietly. 'This is rather an important week for Toby, isn't it?'

'And you.' His tone was soft with something almost like tenderness in the deep depths. 'He means a hell of a lot to you, doesn't he?'

'He's all the family I've got left,' she said simply as she concentrated with fierce determination on the toast, willing the tears that seemed ever ready to fall these days back behind her eyes.

'Yes.' His tone was gruff now and the newspaper was raised abruptly, signalling the end of further conversation, for which she was supremely thankful.

She was just forcing down the last mouthful of toast, having refused the cooked breakfast that Mrs Jones had suggested, when the telephone rang, its note strident. 'Miss Murray? There's a young man on the phone for you, a Mr Hammond?' Even as Mrs Jones spoke she was plugging the phone into the extension in the breakfast-room, much to Angelina's chagrin.

'There's no need for that, Mrs Jones; I could have taken the call in the hall——'

'Nonsense.' The little woman smiled cheerfully. 'You finish your breakfast, dear; I'll pour you another cup of coffee. Here we are.' As she placed the telephone on the table in front of Angelina and passed her the receiver with another smile Angelina took it warily.

'Hello?'

'Angel?' Craig's voice was edged with worry. 'I just phoned the hospital to see if it was OK to bring

Raymond in again this afternoon to see Toby and they told me he's moving up to London this morning. Is anything wrong?'

'Wrong?' Angelina said carefully. 'No, of course not, Craig. You knew we were transferring Toby to Hunter's hospital some time this weekend, didn't you?'

'It just seemed a bit sudden, that's all,' Craig said quietly. There was a brief pause and then he spoke again, his voice hesitant. 'Were you going to let me know?'

'Of course,' she said immediately. 'I intended to ring you this morning after breakfast before we left.' She was acutely conscious of the rigid, immobile body behind the newspaper; the very air seemed to be crackling with electricity, but as there was nothing she could do but try and act normally she continued, 'Toby will miss you, Craig—he's really looked forward to your visits and——'

'And you?' Now the young male voice was probing. 'Will you miss me at all, Angel?'

She hesitated uncertainly. There was a note in his voice that had never been there before—or was Hunter right and she just hadn't noticed the signals for days? She bit her lip anxiously. If Craig did care for her, even a little, there was no way she could encourage him to think he had a chance. It would be too cruel. But after what she'd intimated to Hunter last night the telephone call couldn't have come at a worse time, with the recipient of the lie listening to every word she spoke. 'I'm not sure what you mean,' she prevaricated quietly, jumping as Hunter suddenly rose from the table in one knife-sharp movement that sent his chair skidding back into the wall.

'We leave in ten minutes,' he said abruptly as he passed her swiftly, his face icily remote.

'I'm sorry, Craig,' she spoke into the receiver quickly. 'Hunter's just left the table and——'

'Angel, is he *just* Toby's doctor?' Craig asked softly, his voice faintly apologetic. 'I'm not asking to be nosy but I need to know if there is any chance for me, you understand?'

'Yes, I understand.' She took a deep breath, praying that her answer wouldn't be too much of a blow to the young man who had been such a good friend to her over the last week. 'And I'm sorry, Craig, I like you very much—*very much*—but not in that way.'

'I see.' There was a blank silence for some seconds and she shut her eyes tightly, stricken that she had had to hurt someone who had showed her nothing but kindness. 'Well, I needed to know. I'm sorry if I've embarrassed you.'

'No, you haven't,' she said quickly, 'and it's I who am sorry. I wish with all my heart it could be different, Craig; I hate feeling the way I do at the moment.'

'Is it Hunter?' he asked carefully.

'Yes, but not in the way you think,' she said miserably. 'He doesn't want a serious relationship with anyone.'

'Then he's a fool.' There was a deep, deep sigh down the phone. 'Brilliant, maybe, but a fool. Can I still come and see you when you get back?'

'I'd like that.' She glanced at her watch and spoke hastily. 'I really have to go now. I'll give you a ring when I know more about Toby's chances.'

'Please do. And Angel——' He stopped abruptly. 'I just want to say I'm here, if you change your mind, that is.'

'Thank you, Craig, you're a very nice man,' she said softly. 'I'll ring you later.' As she put the receiver back on its rest she raised her eyes to see Hunter standing in the doorway of his study, clearly having heard the last words she had spoken. As she stared at him across the space of the hall through the open breakfast-room door she took in the dangerous tautness in the big male body, the blackness of his face, and then he re-entered the study, banging the door violently behind him.

They arrived at the hospital without having spoken one word to each other on the way, Hunter driving the powerful car as if the devil were after him, his face dark and reserved.

The journey to London was accomplished with the minimum of discomfort and once Toby was established in a clinically clean room Hunter disappeared almost immediately, returning an hour or so later with an armful of posters that he flung down on Toby's bed with a quick grin. 'Few of your football favourites to brighten up the walls,' he said cheerfully to the young face looking back at him, which was almost as white as the pillow on which he was lying. 'We'll put them up in a minute but first we need to take some blood and do a couple of tests to start the ball rolling. OK, mister?'

'OK.' Toby was more interested in the posters than what was happening to his body and, once the nurse assigned to his personal care had finished, Hunter began placing the posters on the pale green walls under Toby's direction. As she watched him, Angelina had the strangest feeling that her heart was being torn out by its roots, and as the two began to exchange careless laughing banter about their favourite football teams, who were directly opposed in a match that week, she knew she couldn't stand much more. How she was going to bear the torment of seeing him every day for the next few weeks without betraying herself she just didn't know.

A discreet knock at the door revealed a small and very attractive nurse with Toby's lunch. She flashed dark, worshipping eyes in Hunter's direction as she left, her cheeks flushed. Angelina knew a moment's deep gratefulness that the nurse assigned to Toby was middle-aged, dumpy and the epitome of a mother figure, and then caught herself abruptly. It didn't make any difference in the long run; the whole hospital was full of slim, nubile females who would be only too pleased to fall into Hunter's bed with the merest shred of encouragement, and no doubt the world outside the hospital was of the same ilk.

'Lunch?' She caught Hunter's last word and turned quickly, her cheeks flushing pink.

'I said, would you like to come and have some lunch?' Hunter asked smoothly. 'Toby is going to have his meal and then sleep for the afternoon, I hope, so we'll return this evening, OK?' He ruffled Toby's blond hair and the small boy grinned back at once, his hazel eyes already smudged with sleep. 'I want to show your sister where she'll be staying for the next few days.' He shot a long sardonic glance at Angelina. 'My other home.' It was said in such a way that she knew he was remembering her disgust at the fact that he owned two homes, two cars, and she flushed still pinker. That had been before she knew what he was, how he earned his living.

'Thank you.' She tried for cool aplomb but caught the glint of mockery in his gaze as his eyes flashed over her again.

They lunched at a small and very elegant restaurant just a stone's throw from the hospital, but although the food was delicious Angelina found she had difficulty forcing it past the lump in her throat. He sat, his dark eyes stormy and severe, watching her eat, and as they were finishing coffee he leant across the table suddenly, catching the loose knot she had tied her hair in that morning and removing the clip so that the golden mass of her hair cascaded into silky waves on her shoulders. 'What did you do that for?' she asked indignantly as she raised a trembling hand to smooth back the strands from her face.

'Because I wanted to.' His voice was silky smooth now, soft and deep, and she caught her breath as he continued to watch her without moving. 'I've wanted to do all sorts of things from the first minute I laid eyes on you. I want to taste you, feel you at the same time as you are tasting me, have you mindless beneath me as I do things to you that you've never even dreamt about.' She listened without breathing, aware that he was making love to her without even touching a hair of her head but unable to do anything about it. 'I want to take your innocence so that once that door is opened...' He took her hand in his, his touch predatory. 'Once that door is opened and you know what it can be like, you'll want more, much more.'

'Don't,' she whispered in mesmerised fascination, her tone such that he smiled mockingly.

'I want to explore every inch of your body,' he said softly, 'touch it, taste it, find all those secret places that will make you wholly mine.' His eyes moved to her breasts under the thin cotton blouse she was wearing and to her amazement she felt their tips blossom as his gaze touched, a tingling, heavy sensation causing her to redden with embarrassment at her body's betrayal.

'You're talking about sex,' she said harshly, pulling her hand from his so sharply that she felt her wrist protest.

'Well, of course I'm talking about sex,' he drawled slowly, his eyes hungry. 'It's one of those inconvenient little habits like eating and sleeping that is essential to the human race, a somewhat annoying urge at times but essential nevertheless. You're female, I'm male; it's as simple as that.'

' "Me Tarzan, you Jane" sort of approach?' she asked tightly, her eyes flashing blue fire.

'If you like.' The smoky grey eyes imprisoned her angry blue ones. 'Sex is a matter of hormones and basic instincts, that's all. Built into the female of the species is the urge to nest-build, to have a nice little contract to ensure a lifetime of ease for her and her fledglings, which is nature's ultimate result of this somewhat infuriating drive. Romance is a myth, Angelina; the poets' answer to a society that has become too dishonest to recognise its own basic needs.'

'That's horrible.' She moved back in her chair as though trying to escape the silky, cool voice and cynical eyes. 'You can't really believe that.'

Something flickered in the darkness of his gaze and then he smiled mockingly, his eyes hard. 'Why not?'

'Because...' She hesitated, unable to express the feeling that had consumed her as he'd talked. 'Because you just aren't like that, Hunter,' she said slowly. 'I won't believe that. I've seen you with Toby; I *know* you feel far more than you like anyone to know——'

'Rubbish.' The stinging contempt in his voice paralysed hers, and she stared at him helplessly as he signalled the waiter for the bill, his stance authoritative.

Maybe he was as shallow as he insisted? The heat in the pit of her stomach that had sprung into fierce life as he'd talked still persisted, much to her shame. But how could she love someone like that? She couldn't. The answer came on the wings of instinct. There had to be more, much, much more that she would perhaps never know, for him to voice such sentiments and try to live his life by them. But it wasn't the real Hunter.

She stared at him as he spoke to the waiter, the cold cynicism, apparent in every harsh line of the rugged face, chilling her heart. But she had neither the experience nor the confidence to tackle a man of the world like him on his own ground. Maybe one of the cool, sophisticated women that populated his environment would be able to get through to him, break into the fortress he had built round his emotions. But she? She dropped her eyes to her empty coffee-cup as a sick honesty made her face facts. She had never had a chance.

CHAPTER SEVEN

HUNTER'S mouth was hot on hers, savage even as it plundered the inner sanctuary of her mouth with a violent passion that was shattering. As his naked body moved against hers she felt a million different sensations that fired pangs of desire all over her soft shape, a hot, sweet need rising in her that had to have fulfilment. And then his mouth left hers, moving down her body in a shockingly slow path that had her writhing and moaning beneath him, unable to express all she was feeling but wanting more, much more.

She pressed into him, moving her hands over the firm muscled planes of his body, delighting in his male strength and hard, proud arousal that spoke of the passion she was firing in his body.

This was so much better than anything she could have imagined, a mounting, bewilderingly ecstatic pleasure swirling over their tangled limbs as his hands and mouth worked a magic that was unbearable. 'You want me, Angel?' He spoke softly against her damp flesh and she shivered at the sound of his voice. 'Say you want me...'

'Please...' She heard her voice, begging for release from the heat that was consuming her, but still his voice persisted, harder now and colder.

'Say you want me, Angel.' She struggled against the command but he was relentless. 'Say it.'

But she couldn't. There was something telling her, warning her, that she mustn't give in to him, mustn't betray herself. 'No!'

Angelina came out of the dream to the sound of her own voice echoing round the dark confines of the bedroom and found herself sitting up in the bed, her whole body shaking with shock even as the pangs of raw passion the dream had wrought still continued to snake around her body like fire. She had to get control of herself, had to; this was the third time this week that her subconscious had led her into areas that were pure, dark enchantment and infinitely dangerous. She couldn't believe the things she dreamt in the raw light of day; they were too shocking, too humiliating to think about.

And yet... She hugged her knees as she sat swaying amid the ruffled covers. It was natural to want fulfilment with the man you loved, wasn't it? Normal to want to please him? This desire, this persistent, strong desire, was only part of the feeling she had for him. It was compounded of so many things: tenderness, concern, compassion, excitement...

She climbed wearily out of bed, padding across to the small *en-suite* and standing for long, cooling minutes under the shower. But it had to die. Had to become barren, unprolific. And maybe it would? She felt hot tears mingling with the silky water as she lifted her face to the cool flow. But how long would it take?

Hunter's London property consisted of a large first-floor apartment in a wildly expensive part of the capital and was the ultimate bachelor pad. Thick carpets, discreet lighting, push-button control for everything from the curtains to the beds and a massive flower-filled balcony that stretched the whole length of the apartment and overlooked quietly elegant gardens and a beautifully wrought fountain that cascaded into a small pool complete with fish.

And she hated it. Not the apartment exactly—it was too sumptuous and well-thought-out to hate—but the whole idea of his life here. The women that must have frequented the high, exquisitely stylish rooms and, more especially, the handsome master bedroom with its kingsize water-bed and black-marbled bathroom, the fashionable, genteel furnishings that proclaimed wealth and independence from all the normal trials of life, the whole grand, dignified façade that seemed to proclaim that the occupier of this place needed and wanted no woman in his life to interfere with his freedom and autarchy.

This was the fourth night here, and each one had been spent tossing and turning and rising at dawn to breakfast in solitary misery on the beautiful balcony in the warm May sunshine. After establishing her in the apartment, Hunter had informed her, with expressionless face and flat voice, that he had booked into his club for the time she was here to ensure her privacy. She had stared at him, noticing for the first time the lines of strain and exhaustion winging from the corners of his eyes and the hard, firm mouth, and innocently asked why. 'I have my own room and bathroom,' she had said quietly, indicating the lovely guest room that made up the other bedroom of the two-bedroom apartment. 'There's no need for you to leave.'

'Trust me.' His voice had been wry and sardonic. 'Even if I can't trust myself.'

She had understood then and had said no more, her face flushing scarlet. Trust him? If only he knew how little she could trust herself.

And it was worse now, because the more she had got to know him over the last few days, the more frequent and disturbing those glimpses of the other man had become. They had dined together each night, always in a crowd but strangely on their own, and the second night he had told her a little of his background. A late only child of well-to-do parents, he had had a youth that had been easy and problem-free, but when she had asked him about university life and medical school the old remoteness had settled over his rugged features and his voice had been guarded. His parents had died when he was still in his twenties, he had informed her quietly, so he knew a little of what she was feeling. She had stared at him then, searching for something in the dark grey of his eyes, although she couldn't have explained what. But the cool slate gaze had defeated her, letting her see nothing of his soul.

And last night? She thought back to their meal at a beautiful restaurant overlooking the Thames when he had looked at her with such a strange expression on his face that it had chilled her blood. 'I lost a patient today, Angel,' he had said quietly, his eyes haunted. 'Talk to me; it doesn't matter about what—anything...' And she had talked and teased and counted it a victory when some time later the greyness had left his face and he had been able to relax. The incident had touched something deep inside her, bringing a wealth of tenderness to the surface. She would have thought he would be immune to the suffering his work entailed by now, philosophical even, but when he had talked about his patient's family and their overwhelming grief she had seen that he cared, really cared.

She glanced at her watch after drying her hair in the bedroom. Five o'clock, and Hunter wasn't picking her up till eight. Certainly enough time to get her body and mind under control before she had to be with him again. The tests had been proceeding satisfactorily, but Hunter had told her he wasn't prepared to make a decision regarding operating until he had all the data he required, which would be at the end of the week. And today was Wednesday. She fixed herself a cup of coffee and wandered out to the balcony but the chilly morning air, still cool with the faint mist of dawn, drove her indoors again.

The telephone rang at six o'clock and she knew instantly, even before she raised the receiver to her ear, that something was terribly wrong.

'Angel?' Hunter's voice was switched into professional mode, smooth and cool and infinitely comforting. 'Were you awake?'

'What's wrong?' she asked breathlessly.

'There will be a car outside in a few minutes,' Hunter said calmly. 'I would have liked to come myself but I need to get ready for Theatre. Toby took a turn for the worse in the night and I need to operate this morning. If you can come immediately you can see him for a minute or two before he goes down. OK?'

'I'm ready now.' She sat down suddenly in the armchair, her head whirling.

'Good girl.' He hesitated, and then spoke again quickly. 'And don't worry, Angel, I'll bring him through.'

'I know you'll do everything you can but I don't expect promises,' she said quietly. 'You're human, Hunter, not some omnipotent being. Just do your best and that will be good enough.'

'You don't mean that.' There was something in his voice that caught her attention even through the spiralling panic and concern for Toby.

'I do.' There was complete silence for a few moments and then she spoke again. 'I trust you implicitly with him, but you aren't God, Hunter; ultimately the final decision is not in your hands. You didn't even have time to finish the tests, did you?'

'The car will be outside by now.' His voice was strange—thick and husky. 'Get your coat.'

By the time she reached the hospital the first initial calm compounded of shock and surprise had gone and sheer raw panic had her in its grasp. Toby, oh, Toby! She felt such a desperate need to see his face that she was blind and deaf to anything or anyone else, and when she entered his room she was shaking all over with what she might see. But he was lying, dressed in a white nightshirt, with his eyes shut and the heart monitor buzzing gently by his side. He opened his eyes once as she walked down by the side of his trolley to Theatre, but the faint smile he gave her was all he could manage and then the heavy lids dropped again.

'Try to keep calm.' Hunter was in a small side-room and came out to see her briefly, looking strange and alien in his white clothes and mask, his eyes darker still by contrast with the white. 'It will take some time, so don't worry.'

'Hunter——' She caught his arm as he went to leave. 'Thank you.'

'Don't thank me,' he said grimly, his mouth hidden by the mask. 'I don't know if I can save him yet.'

'For trying,' she said simply. 'Thank you for trying.'

'Angel——' As a young nurse glanced over interestedly in their direction he stopped abruptly before taking her arm and ushering her into the small waiting-room where she would stay throughout the long operation. 'Angel, I'm too close to this, too involved.'

'What do you mean?' She stared at him as he ripped the mask off irritably and raked his hand through his hair in that gesture she was beginning to recognise.

'Would you rather have someone else? I can get an excellent man here within minutes.'

'No!' They both recognised the panic in her voice and his eyes softened immediately.

'I'm sorry, Angel, I should be reassuring you——'

'What do you mean, you're too close?' she asked desperately. 'Why should that make any difference?'

'No, of course it won't.' He made to leave but she held him so tightly that he was forced to stand still. 'Don't worry, it's just pre-op nerves—happens every time.'

'What did you mean?' she asked again but he gently detached her hand from his arm, his eyes veiled.

'I need to go and scrub up,' he said expressionlessly. He stood looking at her for one infinitesimally tense moment, and then bent down to kiss her hard on the lips.

'Hunter?' Her voice made him pause at the door. 'This has happened before, hasn't it? Was it with a child?'

'I don't know what you mean.' He turned to stare at her, his face blank.

'You do.' She ran a hand agitatedly through her hair. 'I can see it in your eyes.'

'You *see* a damn sight too much,' he said brusquely, before turning in one sharp movement and leaving the room.

The next few hours seemed to stretch on and on into infinity, but in reality lasted no more than the normal five hours the clock told her had passed. It was noon when Hunter came into the room where she was waiting, her hands tightly clenched together and her eyes enormous as she looked up into his drawn grey face.

'He didn't make it, did he?' she said flatly after one long glance at his tense face.

'He's fine.' He answered almost automatically, exhaustion emphasising the lines of his rugged face. 'He's got a few bits in there that aren't his own now, a couple of valves and so on, but he can tell the kids at school he's got a bionic heart, eh?'

He was trying to make light of it all, to defuse the situation, but instead the enormity of it all made her eyes open wide for one split-second before she broke into a torrent of weeping that surprised them both. And then she was in his arms, sitting cradled on his knee as he stroked and petted her as though she were three instead of twenty-three.

'There, there,' he crooned softly, his big hands that could work with such skill gentle and knowing as they stroked her hair and face. 'It's all right; everything's going to be all right.' And for a minute, just a minute, she thought everything was.

He leant back with her against the upholstered seat, the smell of his aftershave and clean, warm feel of his skin banishing the hospital odour and nightmares, and began to talk. 'There is no reason why Toby can't lead a perfectly normal life,' he said cheerfully, with a perceptibly tender glance at her wet face that did nothing to control the flow of tears, 'and grow into an old and probably extremely active man. He's more than likely to reach his three score and ten, probably with a better chance than most of us, I'd say.'

She nodded dumbly before sliding carefully off his lap and standing to blow her nose determinedly.

'He'll need some care for the next few weeks, of course, and the periodic check-up just to make sure things are behaving properly, but he's old bones material, Angel, take it from me.'

'Thank you.' As she raised limpid blue eyes to his dark, rugged face she saw that he was smiling, and for a moment the force of her love for him was a physical pain that seemed to spear her through. 'No one else but you could have done it.'

'Well, we'll never know, will we?'

'I know,' she said slowly, without emphasis. 'I didn't believe half the stories I heard about you at university, but now——'

'Don't make me into a saint, Angelina.' The tone was suddenly hard and harsh. 'You don't know the first thing about me.'

'I know enough,' she said resolutely. 'You have been kinder than anyone I know to Toby and me——'

'I had the money and the resources.' There was a muscle jerking at the edge of his mouth and she realised with a little jerk of bewilderment that he was angry. What could she have said to make him angry? 'Anyone would have done the same in my place.'

'I don't think so.'

'Well, don't think.' There was something in his voice that made her cheeks burn. 'Just go back to your clean young boyfriend and——'

'Don't talk like this.' She stopped, dragging a hard breath of air into her tight lungs. 'Why can't I thank you for all you've done?'

'You have.' He rose abruptly and left without another word.

What on earth had all that been about? she thought dazedly as she sank back down on to a seat. And what did she do now? Wait here? Go and find someone? That dilemma was solved in the next instant as a bright young nurse came into the room, her fresh, clean face smiling.

'Miss Murray? I understand Mr Ryan has told you your brother's operation was a complete success?' she asked cheerfully. 'He's a wonderful surgeon, isn't he?'

'Wonderful,' Angelina echoed faintly.

'If you'd like to follow me, I'll take you up to Mr Ryan's office,' the girl continued sunnily. 'He's arranged for sandwiches and coffee for you and suggested that once you've eaten you might like to go home for a rest? You won't be able to see Toby until tonight.'

'Thank you, but I'll skip the sandwiches,' Angelina said quickly. 'I'd like to go for a walk and I'll perhaps call in somewhere for some lunch before

I go back to the apartment. I'll phone later to see how things are.'

'Fine.' The girl nodded understandingly. 'Do you good to blow away a few cobwebs.'

It took her over an hour to walk back to the apartment but she needed the time to think, to be alone with no one to interrupt her. It was a beautiful day, warm and sunny, with the sky breathtakingly blue and clear, and as she walked through the crowded London streets she was grateful for the anonymity of the busy city where everyone was concerned with his or her own affairs.

Why had she fallen in love with him? She found herself trying to produce solid reasons but there was none. Maybe it had been triggered by his kindness over her car once he had discovered her circumstances from Dr Mitchell? Or perhaps his gentleness with Toby, his protectiveness towards them both? She pictured the big, masculine body in her mind, the hard-angled face and broad shoulders, the strong, powerful virility that oozed from his aura and caused a potent, hot excitement in any warm-blooded female within a forty-mile radius.

She shook her head at her thoughts, causing a young businessman who was walking by to turn for a second look, his glance admiring the curve of her body under the thin summer dress and the smooth, elegant line of her legs as she walked away.

A discreet rumbling in her stomach informed her that she was hungry and, after stopping at one of the numerous street vendors' stalls to buy a giant hot dog liberally doused with fried onions and sauce, she continued to walk along, eating the food, with the May sun hot on her head and something bubbling in her heart she couldn't give name to.

And then she knew. She wasn't going to lie down under this and just accept that there was no chance for them. She wasn't. He might be a powerful, influential man with an attraction that was lethal, but she had seen glimpses of the real Hunter, the man behind the mask, sensed those odd moments of vulnerability that he hid so well, the sudden tensing of that big body when the desire he had for her sprang into life. And that was a start ... wasn't it? Some couples she knew didn't even have that. But what could she do? How could she remain on the perimeter of his life once Toby was better? And she needed to be around, to break down the cynicism and scepticism that was like a hard shell preventing any softer emotion getting through.

Once she was in the apartment her thoughts continued to race and tumble, exhaustion and an overwhelming relief over Toby setting up a reaction that produced one impossibly crazy notion after another. The release of all her fears, the knowledge that her brother was going to get well, had induced a high more powerful than any chemically produced one.

And then the telephone rang. 'Angel?' It was Dr Mitchell. 'I rang the hospital and spoke to Hunter and he said I might catch you here. I'm so pleased! The man's a marvel, isn't he?'

'Yes, he's wonderful.' Whether it was something in her voice or the words she had chosen she didn't know, but she felt the silence grow on the other end of the line, and then Dr Mitchell spoke again, his voice hesitant.

'You aren't getting involved with him in any way, are you, Angel? I understand you are staying at the apartment alone? As an old friend of your father's I feel a moral responsibility——'

'It's all right, there's nothing like that,' she said quickly. 'He's just been so good, that's all.'

'Right.' There was another pause and then he spoke again. 'Because it would be no good, you understand?'

'Well, no, I don't really.' It was now or never, and the chance to find out more about Hunter was too strong to resist. 'I know he doesn't believe in long-term relationships, but that's about all.' She tried a light laugh but it didn't come off. 'He's a very puzzling man.'

'He's a very bitter man,' Dr Mitchell said slowly, 'and he *is* a man, Angel; he's been around a lot longer than you.' He seemed to hesitate, and then spoke swiftly as though he was in danger of changing his mind. 'I wouldn't like this to go any further, Angel—Hunter is an old friend from way back and in his own way one of the best—but I wouldn't like to see any woman I know getting mixed up with him, and least of all you.'

'Why?' She had to ask, although the sense of foreboding was strong now.

'Because he is a confirmed bachelor, my dear. There was an experience in his youth...' He paused then continued quietly, 'He married when he was still at university, one of the female students he worked with, and the girl was pregnant. I don't think either of them was twenty but that's how things go sometimes. She went into premature labour and a heart condition was diagnosed; she died on the operating table along with the child.'

Angelina was conscious of listening, but there was something drumming in her head that was stopping any feeling.

'He was angry—*very* angry,' Dr Mitchell continued meditatively. 'I guess you could say that through that the world gained a heart specialist second to none, but in the process Hunter lost something; something died, closed off. All the confrontations with the medical world in the early days when he first qualified were directly due to that experience, in my opinion, but through it new frontiers were breached and, as you know, the man is something of a legend. But...' He cleared his throat uncomfortably. 'The women are attracted to him, my dear, and he is no shrinking violet. There have been numerous tales...'

'Yes, thank you, Dr Mitchell.' Her voice was too high and she took a deep breath before she spoke again. 'Well, as I said, there's nothing like that between us. Hunter was quite direct about how he viewed women the first time I met him.'

'Unfortunately that doesn't seem to lessen his attraction with most of your sex,' Dr Mitchell said drily. 'Quite the opposite, in fact. It's made him very cynical, Angel, very cynical indeed. Now, enough of the organ-grinder; give me some details about the monkey.' He was trying to lighten the heavy atmosphere and she rose to the occasion, filling him in on everything she knew about Toby before the conversation ended. And then she walked through to the sumptuous and very masculine lounge and poured herself a large brandy, downing it almost in one gulp although she had never drunk it neat before. The raw alcohol spread through her limbs like fire, steadying her nerves and controlling the trembling that was making her physically nauseous. She poured another one and then seated herself in one of the massive cream leather chairs, staring blankly ahead as she tried to absorb all she'd been told. The high had vanished along with her tentative dreams for the future. It was time to face facts.

The most she could hope to be to him was a temporary amusement, a diversion from the beautiful, elegant women of the world he usually slept with who were no doubt expertly skilled in the art of making love. He would find it entertaining at best to teach her his ways, boring at worst, because she could never hope to compete with women who had had various lovers on which to perfect their technique. He was a sensual, rich, attractive and powerful man, and she must have been mad to think

she could ever hope to interest him even a little—
mad!

She finished the second drink and was surprised
to find that her walk was a little unsteady as she
made her way into the bedroom. She needed to lie
down, to sleep. She had never felt so mentally and
physically exhausted in her life. Even tears were too
much effort.

CHAPTER EIGHT

'*WHERE the hell have you been?*'

Angelina jerked upright on the bed in such a panic that her hand caught the little alarm clock on the bedside cabinet, sending it spinning to crash against the far wall. 'I said, where have you been?'

Hunter was standing just inside the open bedroom door, his eyes blazing and his face as black as thunder. 'I've been phoning here every half-hour since three o'clock. What the hell are you playing at?'

'What?' She raised a shaking hand to her head, flinching as the movement increased the sick headache that had pounded behind her eyes as soon as she'd become conscious.

'Were you out with him?' He glared at her furiously. 'Because if so I'll damn well teach him a lesson he'll never forget. Toby regained consciousness nearly three hours ago; you should have been there.'

'What's the time?' She tried to focus her thoughts, talk coherently, but the thick, muzzy feeling made it impossible.

'Eight o'clock,' he said curtly. 'And I'm still waiting for an answer.'

'I've been here.' She moved back against the upholstered bedhead as reality plunged through the fog. 'I'm sorry, I must have fallen asleep——'

'You don't expect me to believe that?' he asked incredulously. 'Craig was at the hospital this afternoon asking for you. Where did you go?'

'I didn't go anywhere,' she said dazedly. 'I told you, I've been here.'

'That phone has rung and rung,' he said angrily, 'and as far as I know you don't have trouble with your hearing.'

'*I was asleep*!' Suddenly the hot temper that he always managed to ignite flared into being. 'If I weren't I'd tell you. There's no reason for me to lie, is there? I don't have to answer to you about who I see or when?'

'Wrong.' His voice was vicious. 'For the moment you are the mainstay of my patient and *everything* you do is my concern. I won't have him worried or upset by your absence when he needs you. Do I make myself clear?'

'Perfectly.' She glared at him furiously as the last of the muzziness disappeared. 'So I don't sleep or eat or anything else, then? Is that what you are saying?'

'Don't treat me like a fool, Angelina.' His scathing voice flooded her white face with angry colour. 'You weren't here this afternoon because you were gallivanting somewhere with your boy-friend. Now have the courage to admit it.'

'How dare you——?'

'And don't try the injured innocent act either,' he said brutally. 'Craig Hammond came all the way up here to be with you. Do you seriously expect me to believe that you didn't see him?'

'I haven't even *spoken* to him,' she hissed tightly. 'I didn't know he was in London.'

'I don't believe you.' As he turned to leave she flung herself across the bed on her hands and knees like an armed missile, almost falling at his feet before she righted herself to stand in front of him, her eyes narrowed into slits of pure frustrated blue rage.

'And that's it?' she asked heatedly. 'You say you don't believe me and then think you can just leave?'

'This is my house, Angelina,' he said icily as his grey eyes swept over her hot face and tumbled hair. 'I can do what I like.'

'Oh, of course, the great Hunter Ryan!' Pain and bitter hurt was making her voice shrill but she didn't care. 'A law unto himself! I'm so sorry, I forgot for a moment.'

'As long as you don't make a practice of it.' The cold sarcasm was more than she could take and as her hand lashed out to connect with the hard skin of his face the impact stunned them both.

She backed from him, overwhelmed with the horror of what she had just done as he swore softly under his breath without taking his gaze off her, his eyes murderous. And then he moved swiftly and silently with predatory intent, his hands harsh as they pulled her to him, all control gone. 'You are no different from all the rest,' he snarled savagely through clenched teeth. 'You *aren't*.' For a moment it almost sounded as though he was trying to convince himself, but then his mouth was on hers, hot and dangerous, and she began to fight him with all her might because she knew, with a surge of indefinable panic, that she must.

With an expertise that spoke of his familiarity with the female shape he moved her into him, one hand tangling in the rich, silky gold of her hair as the other held the small of her back so that with every wriggle, every movement of protest the hard arousal of his body ground into hers, emphasising her softness against his male strength. He towered over her as he plundered her mouth, his big body passionately lethal, but it wasn't fear that made her continue to fight him but the thick, sweet sensations that were sending her limbs weak with desire.

By the time his hands became a caress rather than a restraint it was too late—much, much too late. She whimpered helplessly as his teeth played with her lower lip, intoxicatingly sensual as they teased provocatively at its fullness, and then his mouth was moving lower, to her throat, where a full pulse was beating in exposed vulnerability.

'So tiny and so perfect...' His voice was thick and husky and excited as it played against her throat. 'I want you, Angel; I want you more than I've ever wanted a woman before.'

Want. That word alone should have been enough to stop the madness, devoid as it was of love or tenderness, but her own love was a drug that had been weakening her for days, a dangerous narcotic that was potentially more lethal than anything man-made.

And she did love him, so much. She would always love him. Would it be so wrong to take this one chance of fulfilment with the man she loved when it would have to carry her through a lifetime of barren nights? Would it? But then his mouth moved still lower to the swell of her breasts and she ceased to think, ceased to exist except in the spiralling tornado that had her sweeping upwards on a mounting urge of intense pleasure.

She had never dreamed that a man's body, his hands, his mouth, could induce such wild, wanton pleasure, but she was experiencing it now, shame-lessly inviting it with her soft cries of desire and arching softness.

'Say you want me, Angel, say it...' His voice was soft and passionate, as unlike the dream as it was possible to be, and her answer when it came was the antithesis of every promise she had made herself, a result of her heart and not her head.

'I want you, Hunter...' She shuddered as his hands explored her with intimate gentleness. 'I love you so much...'

For a moment he was simply still, his mouth and hands frozen, and then she saw something like agonised disbelief replace the raging hunger in his eyes as she raised her head to look into his face. 'No.' His voice was a husky whisper as he put her from him to arm's length, his hands still holding her shoulders in an iron grip. 'You don't know what you're saying.'

'I do.' It was too late to pretend, too late to do anything but tell the truth. 'I love you.'

'*No.*' This time his voice was savage and she would have shrunk from him but for his grasp on her arms. 'You're mistaking physical attraction for something else. It's the patient-doctor syndrome, and with all that has gone before——'

'You aren't my doctor, Hunter.' She tried to keep calm, to control the sick panic that was washing over her at the look on his face. She should never have told him; she had known, she had *known* how he would react, but even her wildest fears were better than this harsh reality.

'But you're grateful.' He was talking quickly, too quickly. She ought to say something, do something to save what little pride she had left, but all she could do was watch as he ripped her apart with his eyes. 'And gratitude is a dangerous emotion I should never have taken advantage of. I thought Craig——'

'I'm not a child.' She drew herself up and away from him, her body rigid and her face stiff. 'I know you don't feel the same——'

'Feel the same?' His voice was a harsh bite of anger. 'You're too young to know what the hell you do feel. An older, experienced man, the fact that I've successfully operated on Toby——'

'Stop it!' she screamed suddenly. 'Just stop it, Hunter. You were only twenty when you married——'

His dangerous tautness as her words registered cut off the rest of the sentence in mid-stream and her eyes widened at the anger consuming every feature of his face. She forgot her dishevelled appearance, the fact that she had nearly given herself to a man who seemed to hold her with nothing but contempt and primitive animal desire—she forgot everything as she watched dark temper dilating his eyes into pools of black rage.

'Yes, I married young,' he said with a curious softness that belied the savage anger, 'but you got one thing wrong. I was nineteen, not twenty. At twenty I was a widower, burying my wife and child.'

'Hunter——' She reached out an imploring hand but his mouth was tightly compressed now, his face as cold as stone.

'And the ironic thing is that within five years of their deaths technology had advanced to a point where the operation involved had become, if not commonplace, then feasible. It just needed one man to forget his damn credibility and reach out.'

He still loved her. She looked into those pewter-grey eyes and read an emotion there that chilled her blood. After nineteen years he still loved her.

'Angelina...' He swept his hand across his face as though to cut out the sight of her. 'Do you want to see Toby tonight?'

'Toby?' Her emotions were such that for a second the name was foreign. 'Yes—yes, of course. But——'

'Then get ready. I'll wait outside in the car.'

The drive to the hospital was a nightmare but she survived it. She also survived the bittersweet hour with Toby, who was a mass of drips and wires, and the drive home with Hunter, who was as cold as a block of ice.

And the next day arrived in spite of her consuming pain and grief, and the next, and the next...

After two weeks Toby's recovery was such that he was allowed home, and within six he was back at school and she was working in the surgery again as though life were normal. But it would never be normal. Her heart had been ripped out by the roots and no one knew...or cared.

The three-monthly check-up was the sort of endurance test on her emotions she wouldn't put her worst enemy through. Hunter was remote and austere, the cool, professional consultant complete with designer suit and hand-made shoes, and even Toby emerged slightly puzzled and woebegone.

'Angel?' Just as she reached the door, her head held high and teeth clenched, Hunter called her back.

'Yes?' She looked into his face, that dear face she would always love—and hate—and managed a cool smile.

'You're too thin,' he said brusquely. 'Eat more.'

'Eat more?' She was too surprised to protest further.

'How's Craig?' he asked expressionlessly. 'Are you two an item now?' He shifted slightly in his seat, his face dark.

'If that's what you want to call it,' she said flatly. They weren't anything at all, but if it relieved his sense of responsibility then so be it. She would never crawl to this man again, never. But he did look good. Her bones had melted as she had walked into the room once Toby had had his examination.

'I see.' The urge to hit him was paramount again, but she had learnt control over the last three months and merely gave a curt nod before turning and leaving the room, her pride intact and her heart bleeding.

The invitation came through Dr Mitchell a few weeks later. It had been a hot August and looked like being an even hotter September. She had taken time to sunbathe for the first time in years, lying in the sun at the weekends for long, lazy hours in a kind of numb dream. She had found it was the only way she could cope with the knowledge that he was out of her life for good. If she tried to acknowledge the mental reality in anything but the odd sharp burst she was useless for anything for days. But she was getting better, she told herself that morning on the way to work, her sun-bleached hair high on her head in a loose knot and her skin the colour and texture of honeyed silk. It had been at least a week since she had cried the night away; that was a definite improvement on those first early days. And Toby was fine. Her mouth turned up at the corners as she thought of her brother, who was transformed into a bundle of energy with a zest for life that was unquenchable.

'Angel?' Dr Mitchell was at his desk as she walked into his office with his morning cup of coffee, a shaft of sunlight from the uncurtained window turning his grey hair to a shock of silver. 'We've all had an invitation.'

'We?' She glanced over his shoulder and then wished she hadn't as her stomach clenched in a giant knot. 'From Hunter Ryan?'

'It would appear he's leaving England for an indefinite period,' said Dr Mitchell in surprise as he read the accompanying letter to the gold-embossed invitation. 'Been offered some sort of high-powered opportunity in America, from what I can make out. I know they've been after him for years. He's throwing a leaving party at the Gables next week and we're all invited, Shelly and Tom included.'

'That's nice.' She was amazed at how calm her voice was. 'What's the date? Oh, what a shame, I'm booked that night.'

'Angel . . .' Dr Mitchell turned to look up at her, his lined face gentle. 'Think before you refuse. I'm not blind even if I am in my dotage. I've seen you these last few weeks and it's hurt me to see you so unhappy. I don't know what went on between you two and I don't want to——' he raised a hand as she went to open her mouth '—but one thing I *do* know. You need to say goodbye to him properly, without any animosity or ill feeling that you'll regret in the years ahead. He *did* save Toby's life—don't lose sight of that. No other surgeon would have attempted what he did on such a sick child. I had the reports through as Toby's GP and Hunter almost rearranged his body.'

'I know.' She shook her head wearily. 'I do understand what he did for Toby.'

'Then give him the chance to go to America with your blessing,' Dr Mitchell said quietly. 'He is as he is, Angel; you won't change him. And you're young; you'll meet——'

'Don't tell me I'll meet someone else.' The sharpness in her voice surprised them both and she reached out immediately, her face apologetic. 'I'm sorry, I didn't mean it to sound like that—but I won't. It doesn't matter, anyway...' She waved her hand tiredly. 'It's all over and done with.'

'Then you'll come to the party?' Dr Mitchell asked again. 'Rose and I will be there, and Tom and Shelly. The invitation says "and partner" so you needn't come alone. What about that nice young schoolteacher who was so concerned about Toby?'

He was going to America. He was going to America. The phrase was pounding through her head as though on a tape recorder. She hadn't realised until this very moment that secretly, hidden in the very depths of her, the hope hadn't died. Loving him as she did, she had thought that somehow, some time, she would see him again and everything would work out. *Fool, fool, fool.* She was conscious of talking to Dr Mitchell, promising him that she would consider the invitation, with her brain on another sphere altogether. It was over, really over, and it had never begun.

Shelly was bubbling with excited anticipation once Angelina had relayed the invitation, immediately undertaking a mental overhaul of her wardrobe and deciding that she had nothing to wear. 'Is he selling the Gables, then?' she asked interestedly, pointedly ignoring the long Friday build-up at the reception desk.

'I've no idea.' Angelina indicated the irate patients, who were eyeing them darkly. 'Shouldn't you . . .?' As her friend darted away to the appointments book she began to sort out medical records for the first patients, but with her mind mulling over Shelly's remark. Would he be selling the Gables? She thought again of the beautiful Victorian mansion, the vast grounds with their abundance of wildlife and wonderful gardens and the house itself, old England in the truest sense, and felt a sharp pang of loss. But it was nothing to do with her. She gave herself a firm mental shake. *He* was nothing to do with her.

By the following Friday Angelina was as tense as a coiled spring. Having allowed Dr Mitchell to accept the invitation on behalf of all of them, she had immediately regretted it, telling herself over and over again that it was the action of a true masochist to torture herself by seeing him again—added to which there was the problem of a male escort.

'I don't understand why you can't ask Craig,' Shelly urged for the third time that morning when the subject of the party came up. 'It's not as if you haven't told him exactly how things are. It would be up to him if he wanted to go or not.'

'But it's hardly fair, is it?' Angelina said softly. 'It's too much like leading him on.'

'Oh, come on,' Shelly scoffed, her face indignant. 'He's a grown man of twenty-four, Angel, and quite able to make his own mind up. You've told him there's no chance of anything romantic and it's going to look dead strange if you turn up on Hunter Ryan's doorstep without a man in tow. The invitation did say "and partner"; everyone will be there with someone.'

'I'll think about it,' Angelina prevaricated quietly.

She was still thinking about it at eight the next night as she drove herself to the Gables. Her innate sense of fair play had ruled out asking Craig to accompany her, and, although there were several other unattached men she could have asked, she hadn't. The thought of being with someone else, dancing with someone else was abhorrent, and at least this way she could make an appearance for an hour or two and then slip away quietly when no one was looking. Toby was staying the night with a friend; she had her own transport; the whole evening was hers to do with as she would. Well, almost.

As she drove into the sweeping drive she had become so familiar with a few months ago her stomach did a nosedive. He had been so cold that last time she had seen him at Toby's check-up, so remote and austere—but maybe that was better than seeing him in an informal setting like this? She should never have listened to Dr Mitchell; he wasn't aware of the real situation, after all. No doubt Hunter couldn't care a jot whether she made an appearance or not, and still less whether he went to America with her blessing.

How on earth had she got herself into this impossible position tonight? She sat quietly for a moment after parking the car and surveyed the other vehicles through the Mini's windscreen with a definite feeling of doom. At least she was unique in her choice of transport. The other cars started at Mercedes and worked steadily upwards! She shut her eyes tightly and then took a deep breath before checking her make-up in the mirror.

She had spent most of the day wandering round the large market town where Toby's school was situated in the vain hope of finding a dress that could carry her through the evening with some sort of confidence, eventually ending up in an exclusive little boutique that had only recently opened and was normally empty owing to the exorbitant prices of the clothes inside. And there she had found exactly what she wanted, the only snag being the price, which equalled two months' salary. But it had been worth it. The dress and knee-length jacket in padded silk were in a delicate shade of ivory, the exquisite cut and texture of the material the only embellishment. When the sales assistant had brought a pair of dangerously high-heeled shoes in the exact shade of the silk material she had nodded her acceptance at once, even if the price did make her gasp.

So here she was. She took another long look at herself and opened the door of the Mini before she changed her mind and went straight back home.

She wouldn't run away, not now; besides, she had given Dr Mitchell her word that she would be here. At least there was no need to lock the door of her car. She glanced at the other vehicles with wry amusement twisting her mouth for one moment. No need at all.

She could hear music as she rang the bell and almost immediately Mrs Jones opened the door, her round face beaming as she saw Angelina.

'Miss Angel!' The little woman appeared genuinely glad to see her, and at that moment in time Angelina needed all the friends she could get. 'You look absolutely lovely, dear—quite breathtaking, if I may say so.'

'If you didn't, I most certainly would, Mrs Jones.' She heard his voice, rich and deep, before she saw him just behind the housekeeper's ample frame and as her heart lurched into overdrive she prayed that it wouldn't show on her face. 'Come in, Angel...' The 'host' smile playing round his mouth was cool but the look in his eyes was anything but. 'Is your young man following?'

'My...?' She caught herself quickly and forced an equally cool smile on her lips. 'A last-minute domestic crisis, I'm afraid,' she lied quietly.

'So you're alone?' A muscle flickered in the hard, arrogant set of his jaw, the grey of his eyes brilliant in the lights that were blazing in the hall. He was dressed all in black, beautifully cut cotton trousers teamed with a thin black silk shirt that set off the big, powerful body to perfection. It made her weak at the knees.

'Yes.' By sheer will-power the smile stayed fixed. 'But I shall leave early, you understand.'

'Not really.' He had taken her arm and she couldn't believe the way her body reacted to the light touch. 'But perhaps you'll have such a good time that you'll change your mind?'

He smiled lazily but it didn't reach his eyes. What was he thinking? she asked herself tensely as he walked with her into the main drawing-room that seemed full to overflowing. And his partner? Her stomach lurched sickeningly. Who out of all these elegant, beautiful women was his partner? The sensation of being at his side, the feel and smell of him, was making her dizzy, and she forced herself to concentrate on putting one foot in front of the other as he led her to a waiter balancing a tray of glasses full of sparkling champagne in one hand. All she needed to make this evening complete was to fall flat on her face.

'There's something different...' He turned her to him as she took her first sip of the effervescent wine. 'I know what it is—you've grown.' He glanced down at her feet, encased in the three-inch heels, and the black eyebrows rose sardonically. 'You can actually walk in those things?'

'Perfectly.' She didn't want to feel like this, she told herself desperately—as though she was going to explode from the inside out. She wanted to be cool, cool and composed...like him. She forced her eyes to meet his, trying to ignore the hot panic that was curling her toes and making her breathless. Just below her eyeline she was conscious of the dark, curling body hair that the first two open buttons of his shirt revealed, and her stomach clenched in a sensual spasm that made her almost gasp. 'Is everyone here?'

'You were the last,' he said softly. 'I'd begun to think you weren't coming.'

'Really?' She tried a light laugh and was rather pleased with the result. 'I'm amazed you noticed I wasn't here, with all these people.'

'Are you? Amazed, that is?'

She wanted to shut her eyes, to blot out the sight of him. He was too close, much too close... A thrilling little shiver snaked down her spine right into her toes. She couldn't bear this; it just wasn't fair. What was he doing? Playing with her? Anger secreted enough adrenalin into her body to bring her head upright and stiffen her back. No way, *no way*. There was no way she was going to be the means of feeding that monstrous ego still more. He could get his kicks elsewhere.

'So you are going to America?' she asked coolly. 'Lucky old you.'

'Lucky old me,' he agreed softly.

'And the house? The Gables? Are you selling it?'

As he reached out and moved a tendril of hair from her cheek with one finger she remained stock-still, although the rage increased. 'I haven't decided yet,' he said slowly. 'That rather depends.'

'On what?' she asked tightly. 'I would have thought everything was cut and dried?'

'Angel——' As he opened his mouth to speak she saw Dr Mitchell raise his hand from the other side of the room and waved back quickly, forcing a smile.

'Excuse me, Hunter.' She had moved away before he had time to react, working her way through the throng of people to Dr Mitchell's side as though she were a homing pigeon even as her cheeks burnt and her eyes blazed. How dared he play with her like that? How dared he? She loathed him, hated him. He was the most egotistical, self-centred, selfish——

'Wonderful party, eh?' Dr Mitchell smiled as she reached them. 'And you look lovely, doesn't she, Rose?'

'Lovely.' Dr Mitchell's small, grey-haired wife smiled her agreement. 'Shelly and Tom are around somewhere. You aren't by yourself, are you, Angel?'

'Well, I shan't stop long.' She forced a reply through lips that were suddenly numb with hurt and pain. 'Craig couldn't make it.'

'Oh, what a shame.' Mrs Mitchell smiled cheerfully. 'Still, I don't expect you'll be short of partners once they start dancing. There's going to be a band on the main lawn later, did you know?'

'No.' Even as she made small talk she was vitally conscious that a tall, dark figure had followed her across the room. 'No, I didn't.'

'I was just telling Angel there's dancing later.' Rose Mitchell smiled at Hunter as he reached their side. 'I'm looking forward to it.'

'Good.' Angelina felt warm fingers close over her elbow but for the life of her couldn't look up at him. 'Save a dance for me, Rose.'

'I will.' As the small woman laughed, Hunter moved Angelina round slightly, allowing the party to surge in between them and the other couple.

'I'd like a word with you, Angel.'

She felt the colour lick a painful course across her skin and prayed for composure. Not again! He wasn't going to proposition her again, was he? Did he seriously think she was going to fall into his arms because she didn't happen to have a partner to-night? Because she'd made her love for him so transparent?

'Yes?' Her eyes were stormy as they met the smoky grey of his. 'What do you want?'

'Not here.' He glanced round him as though the beautiful room full of exquisitely dressed people were repugnant. 'Outside.'

'I don't want to go outside with you, Hunter.' Amazingly, the words came more easily than she had thought, probably because the thick oil of bit-terness spreading through her body had eased their way. 'And shouldn't you be with your partner for the evening? Who is it, by the way?' She glanced with studied idleness round the crowded room.

'I'm afraid I don't have one.'

Her gaze flew to his face and became ensnared with his. His eyes were piercingly intent and very dark, their depths fathomless, and she had the strangest feeling for a moment that he was trying to look into her very soul.

'No?' Angelina laughed hollowly. 'How sad. Well, if you'll excuse me——'

The hand on her elbow tightened painfully. 'No, I won't.' He smiled as someone passing spoke to him briefly, but the grimace was without humour and infinitely cold.

'Let go of me,' she spat angrily. 'I didn't come here to be manhandled——'

'What did you come here for?' he asked softly. '*Really* come for?'

'To wish you well.' She had heard that it was a characteristic of the human race that one could aspire to the odd moment of greatness when the chips were down. She hadn't been sure whether to believe it or not, but now she knew that this was her moment. The last time they had parted it had been without dignity, for her at least, and the humiliation and embarrassment of her profession of love had burnt hotly through the long, lonely nights that followed. 'And to thank you again for Toby's life.'

'Yes, I see.' His eyes had narrowed into grey slits and the dark face was hard and implacable. 'Has Craig proposed yet, Angel?'

'What?' The change in conversation was so absolute that she stared at him wide-eyed, her mouth half-open.

'I said, has Craig Hammond asked you to be his wife yet?' he repeated softly. 'You do remember Craig...?'

'Of course I remember Craig,' she snapped furiously as she reached out and tugged his hand from her arm. 'And I also remember telling you once before that my relationship with him is nothing to do with you.'

'So there is a relationship?' he persisted quietly.

'Yes.' She raised her head and stood very still, her face white and wounded and bitter. Let him believe it, she prayed silently; please let him believe it. This thing had to die, had to be crushed once and for all, and if she let him make love to her as just another of his passing whims she would never get over him. And that was all he wanted. She looked into the attractive, rugged face with angry eyes. It didn't really matter whether he still loved his dead wife or not; her death had damaged him so completely that he carried a stone where his heart should be. Physical gratification was the only thing he cared about, but, damn him—she stared into the dark grey eyes—still she loved him.

'OK.' The sudden capitulation was like a slap in the face, and Angelina stared at him uncomprehendingly as he nodded once before sauntering lazily into the crowd. He'd gone? Just like that? But of course he has, her heart jeered silently. What else did you expect?

CHAPTER NINE

THE next hour crawled by on leaden feet. Angelina was aware of each person Hunter spoke to, every move he made, in spite of there being at least sixty people present, and every time his glance centred on a beautiful female face she wanted to die. And that happened fairly often. She was amazed how brazen most of the women were in getting his attention—which just proved how naïve she was, she thought bitterly as one tall redhead, a little more daring than the rest, reached up and planted a passionate kiss right on his lips on the other side of the room. Didn't their partners mind? The redhead's certainly didn't; in fact he seemed to be treating it all as some kind of joke, laughing uproariously as Hunter said something quietly in her ear before moving out of the woman's reach.

The band had arrived and already couples were dancing on the large lawn. The caterers had the massive barbecue at the far end of the garden well under control, and as Angelina glanced around the thinning room she decided to make her escape through the open French doors and round the side of the house to where her car was parked. She got as far as the patio when a large male hand in the small of her back halted her progress.

174

'Angel?' Just one word, but enough to make her heart pound and her knees weak.

'I'm leaving, Hunter.' She turned to face him, her voice harsh. 'Thank you for a lovely party——'

'Have I told you how beautiful you look to-night?' he asked softly, his voice silky. 'How ravishingly, incredibly beautiful?'

'Hunter——' She stopped abruptly and took a long, deep breath to control her mounting rage. She had to handle this with dignity, with cool maturity. 'Thank you,' she managed at last.

'I want to make love to you right now,' he said quietly as his eyes wandered over her flushed face, her wide, violet-blue eyes luminous in the pale honey-gold of her skin. 'Lay you down on the grass with the heavens above and the earth beneath and take you.'

'I'm going,' she said grimly, her voice trembling with such a mixture of emotions that she couldn't have named just one. How could he do this? How could he?

'Not before we have that talk.' As she moved to the side of the house he lifted her bodily off the ground, one arm round her waist, carrying her past the parked cars and still on into the shadowed darkness where the grass grew thick and spiky under a mass of tall fir trees, ignoring her flailing legs and arms as though they didn't exist and with his other hand tight on her mouth to muffle her cries. 'There are definite advantages that haven't struck me before in falling in love with someone who is so tiny,' he said softly against her ear before placing her down on solid ground, still with his hand over her mouth. 'And are you going to be a good girl and listen now?'

She hadn't heard right, she told herself weakly as he let go of her. She couldn't have. She turned to face him slowly, her head spinning.

'Well?' He eyed her warily, his face relaxing at her stiff nod. 'Good.'

'What did you mean——?'

'You said you'd listen.' He suddenly thrust his hands into his pockets and stepped back a pace, his eyes shadowed. 'I want you, Angel——'

Disappointment, bitter, overwhelming disappointment, surged through her body, cutting the last shreds of her control. 'Want me?' she exploded, her eyes blazing. '*Want me*? So what? You want lots of women, don't you, Hunter?'

'No.' He shook his head slowly. 'No, I don't, not since I met you.'

'I don't care if you want me or not,' she hissed painfully. 'I hate you——'

He moved so quickly that she was taken completely by surprise as she found herself lifted up again, one arm round her waist and his other hand over her mouth in the same position as before.

'I should have known I couldn't trust you to keep quiet,' he said softly against her ear, 'but you *are* going to listen to what I have to say, Angel, and then, if you want to walk away——' There was a brief pause. 'I might let you.' The feel of her back next to his hard body was more erotic than she would have thought possible, that sensation transcending the outrage she felt at his arrogance.

'As I said, I want you.' She stiffened and he gave her a little shake of warning. 'But if you'd let me finish, there is so much more I want to say. I want you, need you, love you more than I would have dreamed possible. Since that first morning you have dominated my days and consumed my nights, and at first I hated you for it, hated you even as I loved you. Can you understand that?'

He set her down on the ground again and removed his hand from her mouth, his other arm round her waist pulling her back against the hardness of his body as his chin nuzzled into the soft silk of her hair on the top of her head. She was glad he couldn't see her face; that was her only defence.

'I don't believe you,' she whispered sadly. It was true—she didn't.

'Maybe not, not yet,' he said quietly, 'but you will. And then you can make the decision whether to walk away or stay.'

'Hunter——'

He cut off her voice by turning her gently round to face him, but she shut her eyes desperately. This was all a game, another of his cruel games that would leave her empty and broken. And she couldn't take any more.

'The first morning we met I wanted you physically, Angel,' he said slowly. 'You fascinated me, so small and so very fierce with a beauty that was quite outstanding. And so I came back for more—

I admit it. I used the car as an excellent ploy both to see you again and to come across as a good guy.' He paused briefly. 'But even then there was something motivating my actions that was outside myself, something I'd never felt before. When I found out your circumstances from Roger Mitchell, it hurt.' She opened her eyes slowly. 'But after our less than harmonious beginning I realised I'd got to take things easy if I wanted you—and I did want you.'

He shook his head wearily. 'But I was still fooling myself that what I felt was just the same as always, that I'd be able to walk away without a backward glance once it was over. And then I saw you at that hotel with another man. I would have liked to hit him, Angel. The poor guy wasn't doing anything to anyone, but the feelings he inspired in me...'

'But when you took me home that night, the things you said——'

'I know what I *said*.' He gestured irritably. 'Believe me, I know. There isn't a day since that I haven't cursed myself. I was still trying to believe that you were like all the others, you see—that a brief affair would suffice. And you told me to go to hell.'

'Hunter, stop this.' She reached out to him, her eyes tormented. 'You don't mean what you're saying and it's not fair; I can't——'

'From that night on I was running.' He wasn't touching her now and she could have moved away. 'Running scared. Doesn't fit in with the macho image, does it?' He smiled without humour, his mouth ironic. 'On the one hand I wanted you so much it hurt; on the other I kept telling myself that to get involved with a twenty-three-year-old virgin was like committing suicide. But I still wouldn't face what was really bothering me: that I'd fallen in love with you, hook, line and sinker. It was more comfortable to call it sexual attraction; that was something I understood. I'd never been in love before, dammit; I didn't even *believe* in such a concept.'

'But your wife?' She raised enormous bewildered eyes to his. 'You must have loved her?'

'Not really.' He raked back his hair savagely. 'This is truth-time, so you might as well hear it all. When I got Jenna pregnant I married her. It was clear-cut in those days and we were just two kids having fun. None of it seemed real. Then, just before she got ill, it hit me what I'd done, what *we'd* done. I was nineteen and saddled with a wife and soon to be a father. I was going to have two people depending on me, and suddenly the responsibility was overwhelming. I didn't want it, and Jenna sensed that, although nothing was said. When she died . . .' He shook his head slowly. 'The guilt and remorse and self-disgust were too much to cope with. I hated myself; I hated the fact that mixed up with all the other emotions of regret and sorrow and grief was relief. But it was there.'

His eyes were haunted as they stared into hers. 'Now what do you think of me? I needed a scapegoat to get through, so I blamed the medical profession for not trying hard enough. And I decided, as atonement if you like, that I'd go the extra mile, do what couldn't be done, consider the patient and only the patient and damn the system.'

His dark eyes were depthless as they stared into the past. 'And women—women would be for one purpose only. I'd never get involved again, never be accountable for someone else's happiness. *I* would be in control of my life and, if I messed up, the only person who would get hurt was me. Because I must have hurt Jenna; that's what I couldn't live with for years.'

'Did she say that?' Angelina asked softly.

'No.' The tortured gaze returned to her from the old memories. 'No, she didn't, but in the final analysis there wasn't time. We thought——' He stopped abruptly. 'We thought she was going to be OK, you see; they didn't tell us the true situation before the op. In fact I'd go so far as to say the doctor lied.' Hence his rigid refusal to dress up the stark facts with Toby or anyone else, she thought understandingly. 'There was so much that went wrong at that time, Angel.' He brushed a shaking hand across his face. 'My parents died within a year or so of Jenna and I just didn't want any more grief, any more of getting close to another human being. So I began to choose my friends, and my women, accordingly. And for nineteen years it worked like a dream.' His mouth twisted sardonically.

'And then a spitting little bundle of golden fur exploded into my life and blew it apart. I was vulnerable again. Me, Hunter Ryan. I couldn't handle it, Angel.'

'But you wanted me to marry Craig?' she asked faintly as she felt her hold on the situation slipping. 'You *told* me so.'

'I'd have killed him first.' He eyed her darkly. 'Every time I saw him anywhere near you, the urge to throttle him was overpowering, but I could see he was everything that was right for you—young, clean, untouched by life. But then the noble intentions flew out of the window at the thought of him actually *touching* you.' He turned from her then, his face in profile and his body stiff and taut.

'That evening when I lost my head and you told me you cared, it scared me.' His voice was full of biting self-contempt. 'Up until then I'd kidded myself that you were interested in Craig Hammond; that although we had some sort of sexual response between us neither of us was in too deep. Crazy, eh?' His face was drawn and tense. 'I wanted to believe that you were just like the rest, Angel; that we could enjoy each other for a time, that I could rid myself of this obsession I had with you. But...' his mouth twisted '...I'd forgotten how narrow my world is, that there are thousands of people who still have ideals they live by, die by if necessary. And you're one of them.'

Somewhere deep inside the hope was flowering, a fierce joy welling up that was taking possession of her senses. His face was still tense and tight, his eyes piercingly resolute, but there was a vulner-ability, an exposed defencelessness in his stance that she sensed he found it difficult to let her see. But he was letting her see it.

'I've been a fool, Angel, and I don't deserve you, I know that. I don't know if you still care, but I know you aren't involved with Craig Hammond, so if you lied about that...' His voice trailed away. 'If you lied about that, it might be because I haven't killed your love completely.'

'How do you know I'm not seeing him?' she asked faintly.

'I know everything you've done, everyone you've seen over the last few weeks,' he said without the faintest trace of apology. 'Since the day after Toby's operation, in fact. I still couldn't quite believe that you meant it all, that someone like you could love a man like me.' He shook his head slowly. 'I walked out of that apartment and nearly went crazy waiting for you in the car, and when you came you were so cool, so untouchable and I knew I'd blown it.'

'But you were so cold,' she whispered slowly. 'You didn't seem to care——'

'I cared.' He shut his eyes for a split-second and in that moment she knew all her instincts had been right. The real Hunter was made up of so many facets, of which the hard, severe exterior was just a tiny part. She had been right to love him; *she had been right*!

'Within days I got the offer from America, but there was never any chance of my accepting it. I couldn't be so far from you; even if it was all over I had to keep trying, somehow. I had faced the fact I'd been running from since the first moment I saw you: that I loved you, that you meant everything to me. If you'd flown into Craig Hammond's arms I honestly think there would have been murder done, the state I was in.'

He eyed her with an endearing air of discomfiture. 'But you didn't, and that fact alone kept me going when I thought I'd killed your love. Hell...' He groaned softly. 'I couldn't work, I couldn't sleep, and when I contacted Roger he wouldn't discuss you, warned me off, in fact, until I told him about the offer from America. When he thought I was going to be several thousands of miles away within weeks, his whole attitude changed.' He eyed her wryly. 'You do inspire deep emotions in men, Angel.'

'He looks upon himself as a father figure now,' she said quickly, 'and he doesn't approve of——' She stopped abruptly.

'Of my lifestyle?' Hunter finished sardonically. 'No father would. And so I dreamed up the idea of this damn party even though I'd already refused America.' He shifted slightly, his shoulders tense.

'The party is for me?' she asked weakly. She would have to sit down soon, she really would; her legs seemed to have the consistency of melted jelly.

'If you had refused the invitation, I intended to use it as an excuse to see you and ask why,' he answered quietly. 'And if you accepted, I was going to see you anyway. Either way, I was going to ask you to wear this.'

As he drew the tiny box out of his pocket the look on his face wrenched her heart. There was a susceptibility there, a little-boy-lost look in the grey eyes that seemed to leave him wide open, and suddenly she realised he wasn't sure how she would react. The great Hunter Ryan was as nervous as a kitten.

'If you accept it, it's the third finger of your left hand,' he said softly as she raised the lid to expose the beautiful star of flashing diamonds on their ring of gold. 'And with it is my heart. I love you, Angel; I love you more than any man has ever loved a woman.'

'You're asking me to marry you?' she whispered in amazement, the melting jelly moving swiftly into every part of her body.

'I can't live without you,' he said simply. 'I don't want to try to for another second, another minute, and this is in the cold light of reason without my having touched you. If I touch you I can't think straight. I want to take care of you and Toby, worry about you, love you. I want it all, Angel, even the damn roses round the door.'

'Hunter!' She leaped into the arms that reached out instinctively to receive her and then she was held close against his broad chest as he smothered her face in kisses before devouring her mouth in a frenzy that spoke of his total loss of control. And then he stiffened, unwinding her arms from his neck and moving her a few inches away, his mouth rueful.

'You see?' he asked softly. 'No control. But I need to tell you this, Angel, in case you ever doubt me, ever wonder if the marriage bond was an act of possession on my part, a need for your body and a warning to the other Craig Hammonds out there. It *is* both those things, but much, much more. I want to make love with you *because* I love you. I want to feel my child inside the warm swell of your stomach, be there for you, grow old with you. I want to hold you close to me night after night, after hours of making love, and watch you sleep. I want to do a thousand and one little intimate things with you that make up the daily routine of living, and all because I have the right. I want to be your husband, Angel; I want it more than I've ever wanted anything in my life.'

'And I want to be your wife,' she whispered quietly, her eyes blazing with love. 'I love you, Hunter. I always will.'

'What are you doing?'

'I'm writing a letter.' Angelina smiled up at Hunter as he walked stark naked out of the bedroom of their beautiful Caribbean bungalow, his walk lazy and proud and his big, muscled body rippling with the sensual power that took her to heaven and back. 'One of the disadvantages of a special licence is that no one got to know we were getting married.'

'I couldn't wait.' He eyed her darkly, his voice a low growl. 'And while we're on the subject...' He bent over and lifted the thick mass of golden hair from her neck, kissing it so thoroughly that she turned round in the seat of the little writing-desk and lifted her arms to his embrace, smiling as he pulled the silky nightdress over her head to reveal all of her young, supple body.

'Shouldn't I finish the letter first?' she teased provocatively, revelling in the desire his naked body revealed. 'And they'll be bringing our breakfast soon——'

'This is the honeymoon cottage,' he warned imperturbably, his hand capturing one small, perfect breast as he knelt in front of her, the other pulling her into him with a gentle force that was irresistible before his mouth traced a sensual path over the erect nipple. 'They expect to have to wait sometimes.'

As his hands stroked a leisurely trail down the silken, honey-gold length of her thighs, Angelina felt herself begin to shiver and he raised his head briefly, his eyes wickedly satisfied at her reaction to what he was doing to her, before standing and lifting her from the chair and carrying her over to the huge four-poster bed that occupied most of the bedroom.

'Hunter?' She nuzzled her head against his throat as he walked. 'This Angel does have wings, you know. Every time you make love to me I fly into another world where the only thing that matters is us. I love you so much.'

He hugged her to him, the feel of her soft nakedness against the hard-muscled planes of his chest intoxicatingly erotic as he took her lips in a long, hard kiss that seemed to draw her very soul.

'I can't believe we've been here three days,' she murmured dreamily as he placed her on the soft covers, 'or that I'm really the wife of Hunter Ryan.'

'Then I'll have to convince you,' he growled softly, his eyes as hot and fierce as his arousal. And he did, wonderfully, as the letter drifted unnoticed to the floor in the slight breeze from the open window.

Dear Vicky,

You'll never believe where I'm writing this letter from or what I've got to tell you, so, if you're standing up, find a seat before you read on. You know I said in my last letter that nothing ever happens in Braybrook and that my life was mapped out for years ahead without the chance of anything changing? Well . . .

"All it takes is one letter to trigger a romance"

Sealed with a Kiss—**don't miss this exciting new mini-series every month.**

All the stories involve a relationship which develops as a result of a letter being written—we know you'll love these new heart-warming romances.

And to make them easier to identify, all the covers in this series are a passionate pink!

Available now   **Price: £1.90**

MILLS & BOON

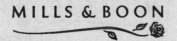

Especially
for you
on
Mother's Day

**Four new romances for just £5.99—
that's over 20% off the normal retail price!**

We're sure you'll love this year's Mother's Day Gift Pack—
four great romances all about families and children.

The Dating Game · Sandra Field
Bachelor's Family · Jessica Steele
Family Secret · Leigh Michaels
A Summer Kind of Love · Shannon Waverly

Available: February 1995   Price: £5.99

MILLS & BOON

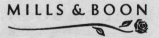

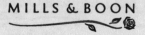

GET 4 BOOKS
AND A MYSTERY GIFT

Return the coupon below and we'll send you 4 Mills & Boon romances absolutely FREE! We'll even pay the postage and packing for you.

We're making you this offer to introduce you to the benefits of Reader Service: FREE home delivery of brand-new Mills & Boon romances, at least a month before they are available in the shops, FREE gifts and a monthly Newsletter packed with information.

Accepting these FREE books places you under no obligation to buy, you may cancel at any time, even after receiving just your free shipment. Simply complete the coupon below and send it to:

HARLEQUIN MILLS & BOON, **FREEPOST**, PO BOX 70, CROYDON CR9 9EL.

- ✂

Yes, please send me 4 Mills & Boon romances and a mystery gift as explained above. Please also reserve a subscription for me. If I decide to subscribe I shall receive 6 superb new titles every month for just £11.40* postage and packing free. I understand that I am under no obligation whatsoever. I may cancel or suspend my subscription at any time simply by writing to you, but the free books and gift will be mine to keep in any case.
I am over 18 years of age.

NO STAMP NEEDED

1EP5R

Ms/Mrs/Miss/Mr _____

Address _____

_____

_____ Postcode _____

mps
MAILING
PREFERENCE
SERVICE